secrets lies & LOCKER 62

Praise for Lil Chase's *Boys for Beginners*:

'A warm and funny story for 10+ readers about friendship, family and growing up'

Guardian

'Hilariously and charmingly, Gwynnie tells her own journey of discovery'

Julia Eccleshare, lovereading4kids.co.uk

'Very funny . . . realistic and scarily relatable'

Wondrous Reads

'An entertaining story, light-hearted and sweet . . . a great debut novel from an author who is definitely one to watch'

Bookbag

Also by Lil Chase

Boys for Beginners

secrets, lies & LOCKER 62

LIL CHASE

Quercus

First published in Great Britain in 2012 by

Quercus
55 Baker Street
7th Floor, South Block
London
W1U 8EW

A CIP catalogue record for this book is available
from the British Library

ISBN 978 0 85738 483 6

1 3 5 7 9 10 8 6 4 2

Printed in Great Britain by Clays Ltd, St Ives plc

For my dad:
you allowed your children to jump off high ledges
but only once you'd checked the water was deep enough.

Prologue

I can't believe what I've just done.

The girl who ran through the halls of Mount Selwyn High School was still in shock, her hair still wet from the shower. It was way past eight p.m., five hours since it all started, but everyone had left for the day and no one had seen.

She took the stairs two at a time and she went into the basement. Her locker was tucked away at the side, in a dark enclave with just a few other lockers. People only walked this way if they had to get to the music rooms, but it was too late even for after-school classes.

She'd had no choice. She'd had to do it.

Or did I?

At her locker she scanned left and right before she opened the door and pulled out her backpack. She shoved in her school fleece, her gym socks — they might keep her warm if she had to sleep rough for the night – her favourite book of poems and one exercise book. On the front was written:

Hillary Randle
Mr Holt's Form
Lower Sixth

No one understood what it was like to be her: Head Girl, Hockey Captain, Netball Captain, Founder of the Poetry Club. All her life she'd tried to be perfect, and she'd failed. If anyone knew the truth, if her parents knew what she'd done, they would disown her.

But now only one thought circled and circled in her mind:

Have I killed her?

She ripped out pages of work from the book: grade A, after grade A, after grade A, fell to the floor. Then she stopped and ripped out a blank page and wrote on it:

I am a coward

She paused as she realized she hadn't said the most important thing:

and I love you.

She folded the note in half and placed it on the shelf of the dark blue metal locker.

A noise startled her. Someone else was in the building!

She quickly put the book in her bag, clipped the bag shut and slung it over one shoulder. With tears in her eyes she said goodbye to the school, and to her life.

Then she closed the locker, locked it and walked quickly down the hall to the fire exit.

It was locker number 62.

Chapter 1

I'm starting a new school today and I can't wait!

Because of Mum I have to wait a bit longer than I want to. Registration is already over so we're going straight to my first class.

'Here we are!' says Mum.

The science lab. Great. My first lesson is my worst subject.

'Lipgloss pep talk!' orders Mum, and pulls a Juicy Tube from her pocket. She smoothes it over my lips and I rub them together. Then we look each other in the eye and both say, 'Cool is everything!'

Mum starts sniffing, and I see she's crying. Actually *crying*! I rub her arm. 'Come on,' I say. 'This is not time for Mum the Hormone Monster.'

'I'm just sorry you're going to be late,' she says. 'I couldn't get it together this morning. Must be the bumpling.'

'Don't try and put this on the pregnancy,

Mum,' I say, pointing down at her round belly. 'You've always been disorganized!'

Mum puts her hands up. 'It's a fair cop, guv,' she says, laughing back the tears. She tucks a strand of her curly brown hair behind her ear. 'I think you're allowed to be late on your first day,' she says. 'In fact, it's kind of expected. Now all your new classmates will think you're a rebel.'

'I'm not a rebel,' I tell her.

'Yeah, I know. But it might be fun to reinvent yourself – become a cool girl for a change. Make all the other kids *want* to hang out with you . . . for a change . . .'

'I'll be, like, the most popular girl in school?'

Mum nods.

'I like the sound of that!'

'You're so beautiful, darling. And with that snazzy new haircut and those funky red tartan tights that go with your new red uniform, you'll have everyone falling at your feet this time.'

One of the good things about Mum is that she's not afraid to spend money on me. She wanted to give me the best start in my new school – especially as I'm joining Mount Selwyn in mid-October and I'll be at a school with actual boys, sitting and learning in the same class as me. So we went to the swankiest hairdressers in London, flicked through tons of mags and chose the latest cut going. We dyed my hair from its normal blonde to brown like Mum's and cut it in a short-short boy-cut. The magazine said it's going to be the NBT – Next Big Thing.

I am no longer blonde, gawky Maya Andrews with a bump in her nose, a slightly unhealthy interest in books and only one friend in the world. I am mysterious and alluring Maya Andrews, with a secret and interesting past, who's cooler than cool.

That's the idea, anyway. *Mum*'s idea.

Mum sniffs again and flaps her hands in front of her face. 'I'll walk you in, shall I? Maybe I'll recognize your teacher from the good old days.'

'No!' I say, too quickly and too loudly. I look at Mum and wince.

She laughs. 'Of course you don't want me in there spoiling your street cred.' She kisses me on the cheek and I pull her in for a hug.

'Don't break too many hearts,' she says, then walks away.

I wait until she's out of sight before I reach for my mobile and send Frankie a quick text.

About to go in. Wish me luck x x

I only have to wait two milliseconds for

Frankie's reply:

Gluck darling. Remember what we talked about: mysterious and alluring. And remember that you always have your beffy x x

I text her right back:

Thanks, Beffy. See you after school tonight x x

Deep breath. This is it. First impressions are everything, and I really want to make Mum proud. As soon as I open that door I have to be cool . . . and pretend cool comes naturally.

I plaster a gigantic winning smile on to my face, lift my head up, chest out, and walk in, trying not to look too much like a rooster. The whole class, teacher included, turns and looks at me.

'Hello,' says the teacher, a man who looks like Jim Carrey, if Jim Carrey had a sweaty face and a weird dress sense. 'Can I help you?'

I am momentarily stunned by the sixty or more eyes on me. I see thirty students wearing shirts with tartan ties and red jumpers with the Mount Selwyn school crest at the top left. We wore grey woollen V-necks at St Cecilia's, with green checked shirts. This looks completely different. But I snap out of it quick and say, 'Hi, I'm—'

'The Year 7s are on the floor below. Would someone—'

Year 7! 'No, I – er – I . . . I'm Maya Andrews. I'm starting Year 9 today.'

Perhaps a slightly false start. There are a few titters from around the classroom. It's happening again.

'Of course you are. Maya Andrews.' He ticks my name on the register. 'I'm Mr Holt. Grab a seat.'

The lab is set out in long desks for doing experiments, with about six stools to each desk. I see there are two free stools for me to choose from. The first is next to a girl with perfect make-up, blonde ringlets and an expression that says she doesn't want to be here. She's leaning sideways and whispering to an equally beautiful girl with black hair extensions in neat cornrows that fall into large curls. These two are clearly the popular crowd, and to make the most friends I have to hang out with them.

There's also a space next to a nutty-looking girl dressed as a goth. She has olive skin with so much make-up on that she needs a Wet Paint sign. Her foundation is pasty white and she has black eyeliner all around her eyes. Her uniform looks like everyone else's, but her tights are ripped, clearly on purpose, and she's drawn a dagger on her notebook sticking out of the word *Chemistry*. Um, it's not that I'm opposed to goths in general, but I don't think she and I would have anything in common. Besides, I want to be the coolest, most popular girl in the school, and I don't think that's going to happen sitting next to her.

Then I see there would be one advantage – one *gorgeous* advantage – in sitting next to the goth girl: the most super-hot guy I've ever seen in real life. He has wavy brown hair, big brown eyes and cherry red lips. I walk towards his desk and smile at him as I pass. Then, with sudden bravery, I say, 'Hi.'

He nods his head at me and does a half-smile. 'Hi,' he says.

Five minutes into my first day and I think I have developed my first crush.

I pull back the stool next to goth girl, but the amazingly gorgeous boy is still looking at me. OK, *mysterious and alluring, mysterious and alluring. Cool is everything*. I give him a mysterious and alluring look. He laughs a little. Not the result I expected, but still a result.

I go to sit down, trip over goth girl's gigantic backpack . . . and fall flat on my bum.

Smooth, Maya. Very smooth.

The class bursts out laughing and continues to laugh solidly for about five minutes. I haul myself up from the floor and try to laugh along with them. It's a trick I learned at my last school.

'Too busy staring at Ben Sands to concentrate?' says Mr Holt. 'What's your name again?' he asks me, and probably because of the hideous humiliation, I completely forget what my name is. I'm not sure forgetting your name counts as being mysterious.

'Err . . . Maya Andrews,' I finally say.

'If you . . .' he starts, then, 'Wait a minute . . . Maya Andrews?'

Here it comes. I knew it would happen eventually but I hoped it wouldn't happen in the first lesson of my first day.

'Are you Leanne Andrews's daughter?'

'Yes, sir.' I nod.

'Well, I never!' He says it like this is more exciting than Madonna being my mum. Or *the* Madonna being my mum. 'Let me tell you something, class. Leanne Andrews was quite a hellraiser at this school. What a reputation she had!'

Everyone says, '*Ooooo*,' like my mum is a big deal. The two cool girls turn to look at me again.

I try to smile. The one with the ringlets raises her eyebrows.

'And as well as being notorious at Mount Selwyn, Maya's mother has written lots of scientific papers on the copulation of rats.'

The room sighs. They thought my mum was going to be interesting.

'Don't look so disappointed,' he says. 'Copulation means sex.'

The fact that a teacher has just used the word *sex* means everyone is laughing. At me. Again.

I slap my face with my palm.

Mr Holt hands me a textbook and tells me to turn to chapter seven. Everyone is working in silence so I take the opportunity to assess my new class. At the back there is a gigantic, terrifying-looking boy. He's the only person wearing a jacket over his uniform, an army jacket. I'm sure I can see stubble on his chin. He looks much older than everyone else. In front of him is—

'Karmella!' shouts Mr Holt.

All heads turn to look at the cool girl with the blonde ringlets.

'Karmella, what's that in your hand?'

'Nothing, Mr Holt,' Karmella says.

'It's not nothing. Give me that piece of paper.'

'It's my diary, sir,' she says, looking defiant but also a bit scared.

'It's not your diary, Karmella. And if it is, you shouldn't be writing it in class.' He snatches the piece of paper out of Karmella's hands. 'If it's so important, I'm sure the whole class should hear.'

Everyone in class hates this bit; we're all feeling Karmella's pain. He reads the paper aloud. 'Vote on the new kid: male or female or a tragic . . .' Mr Holt tails off as everyone starts laughing.

Oh God! I'm blushing like mad and starting to sweat. Maybe my new short-short boy-cut is not the Next Big Thing; maybe it's a Long Way Off. And I'm sure the bright red sweaty look will never be trendy.

Mr Holt growls at Karmella. 'Karmella, you are in a lot of trouble—'

'But, sir,' Karmella protests, 'I didn't start the note. Look, there were loads of ticks in the "Tragic Posh Idiot" column before it got to me.'

'I don't care who started it. You're the one being punished.'

'But, sir. That's so un—'

'It's OK, Mr Holt,' I say, not wanting to make enemies on my first day, especially not with a girl like Karmella. 'I'm sure it was only a joke.'

Mr Holt ignores me. 'Karmella, I want you to look after Maya. Make sure she gets to her classes, show her where the toilets and the changing rooms are, and make her feel welcome.'

Someone shouts, 'Gutted, Karm!'

Hanging round with me has just become a punishment. I have to think of a way to turn it into a perk. Then maybe I can get into the cool group after all. Then maybe I won't be bullied again, like I was at my last school.

Chapter 2

'It was so hideously unfair of Mr Holt to punish you.'

I'm walking down the corridor with Karmella and the other girl, the one with the cornrows and hair extensions. I'm still carrying my coat, gym kit and all my stuff as I didn't get the chance to put it away before class.

'*Hideously!*' the other girl scoffs.

Hideous was what everyone said at St Cecilia's High; apparently it hasn't made it to London yet. Or maybe *hideous* was last year's word and it's completely over.

'Don't be rude to the new girl, Roche,' says Karmella, and Roche looks shocked. 'Maya, this is my best friend, Rochelle.'

'Hi,' says Rochelle.

'Hi!' I say. 'Rochelle is such a pretty name.'

Rochelle smiles.

Wow, that was easy! Friends with the cool crowd on my first day.

Karmella looks at Rochelle, winks at her, and then stops walking.

'Just so you know, this is the ladies', and I need to go.' Karmella continues: 'Roche, didn't you say you needed to go too?'

'I'm absolutely desperate, dahhhhling,' she says. I think she's mocking my accent.

They push on the door to the ladies and I'm about to follow them in when Karmella says, 'We'll only be a sec. Will you wait for us out here?' And they head inside.

I watch as everyone walks by, most of them ignoring me but some giving me a look because I'm clearly new and they don't know why I'm standing outside the girls' loos like a lonesome lemon, carrying all my things. I hope no one tries to pick on me before Karmella and Rochelle get back. My tartan tights were so cool in St Cecilia's, but everyone here is wearing sheer black ones. Their school skirts are rolled up really short.

I try to subtly roll mine up too.

Gradually the corridor clears. I look at my watch; they've been ages and our next class is in five minutes.

I decide I can't face being late twice on my first day — I know it's sad, but I can't fight my nature. I push the door to the ladies' and I am instantly hit by the smell of bleach and cigarette smoke. It's quiet.

'Karmella? Roche — er — Rochelle?'

No response. Nothing.

There are five cubicles on either side and I walk down, pushing the doors. All ten are empty. At the far wall there is another door, tucked behind a cubicle, and when I push that door I see it leads out into a different hallway with classrooms leading off it.

They must have left this way. They forgot I was waiting for them.

Now I have only four minutes to find my locker and dump my stuff. So it looks like I'm going to be late. Again.

A beep from my phone:

How was the first lesson? Fall for anyone yet?

Frankie. Who else? I text her back:

Head over high heels! Will tell all tonight, got to find my locker then head to English.

She replies:

How romantic! Love at first lesson.

I open the printout the receptionist gave me

16

with my timetable, my locker number and a map of the school.

Maya Andrews: Locker 62.

According to the map, it's downstairs in the basement so I follow the crowd and head there. There are rows and rows of lockers all side by side and back to back. Mine must be here somewhere. Each of the lockers looks the same; metal, painted blue, with a combination lock and three tiny slits for air vents.

But lockers 61–70 aren't here with the others. The numbers lead off to a little enclave round the corner from the lunch room. I run back there, ducking and weaving through the hoards like a rugby player. The bell rings for the start of the next lesson, but it will take me one second to shove my stuff away and then I can go.

My heart sinks as I finally get to my locker. My mum once took me to Jimi Hendrix's grave in Paris and this locker has about the same amount of graffiti. People have scratched hearts into the blue paint and written all over it. There's things like:

'*What happened to you?*'
'*Where'd you go?*'
'*We miss you.*'
And,

'It turns out we all have secrets.'

I put in the code. The door doesn't open. I try again. Oh no, please don't say they've given me the wrong combination! I look around to ask someone to help, but everyone has gone to their next class. Reading the code once more, I carefully dial in the right numbers. Then I use all my strength to pull the door open.

It's worked!

Argh!

Thousands of little pieces of paper come pouring out and I have to slam the door shut to stop a real mess. Lucky I have ninja-quick reactions. Is my locker the school's rubbish bin?

My quick response wasn't quite quick enough to stop about forty bits of paper falling around my feet. I scoop them all up and see that each one has something handwritten on it. One of them says:

I'm not scared that my dad will die in Iraq, I'm scared he'll come back and won't be the same.

That's really sad. Who wrote this? I pick up another one and see the handwriting's completely different.

I feel so ugly that sometimes I cry in the toilets.

Is this a message for me? I must teach her the lipgloss pep talk.

My family will kill me if they ever find out I'm gay. I'm going to try my best not to be gay any more.

I have to help this person, let them know that there is nothing wrong with being gay.

But not now: now I have to get to English before I miss it completely.

I text Frankie:

My locker doubles as a trash can!

She texts back:

Whoa! Severe funding cuts! ☺

Finally, all done. Congratulations to me. Oh,

there's one more piece of paper that's fluttered further away. I pick it up and read it. It's written in purple ink, and there's a star instead of a dot over one of the i's.

I passed the note about the new girl. I want karmella to be MY friend, not her friend. The new girl is so tragically uncool.

I feel sick.

Chapter 3

Someone has started a hate campaign against me. It's like St Cecilia's all over again! They passed that note, then came straight to my locker and put this message in here. Did they want me to find it?

But that's not the real problem. The real problem is that I am '*tragically uncool*'.

I hear a gasp from behind me and hide the note behind my back.

'What do you think you're doing?!'

A girl emerges from the darkness of the corridor.

'I . . .' Once she steps closer I see that it's the goth girl, and she's carrying her enormous backpack. 'I'm cleaning out this locker,' I tell her.

'You can't. That's sacrilege. Do you know how many people care about this locker and what it represents?'

From the way her painted eyebrows dance up and down her forehead I can see she's genuinely angry with me.

'This locker represents a place for me to put my stuff,' I tell her.

'We all have baggage we need to offload,' she says, 'or else we'll go mad.'

I wonder if the *'going mad'* ship has already sailed for this girl. 'Yeah,' I say, 'I've been dragging this stuff with me and it's been making me insane. Not to mention the pain in my shoulders.'

'These things can weigh us down, can't they?' she says with a nod.

'Exactly,' I nod back, motioning to her backpack that looks like it weighs over a ton. 'Like books and a PE kit.'

'Bottling up your secrets is unhealthy –' She pauses and frowns at me. 'What did you say? What's this got to do with PE?'

'What did *you* say?' I ask. 'What's this got to do with secrets?'

She pokes her head forward and looks at me as if I have problems speaking English. 'You do know what this is?' she asks, pointing to my locker.

'This. Is. My. Locker,' I explain, and slowly, just in case she has learning difficulties or something.

'This isn't your locker,' she says. 'It's locker 62.'

'Yes, locker 62 . . . my locker.' I wave the printout the receptionist gave me.

Goth girl's mouth drops wide open and her eyes look like heavily made-up saucers. She grabs the slip from me and reads it, but she still looks doubtful. 'Prove it,' she says.

I dial in the code and open and shut the door quickly so no more paper falls out.

'I'm speechless,' she says. 'Which is possibly a first.' She shakes her head slowly. Then, slightly more agitated. 'Have you read any?'

I'm sensing from her reaction that something huge has just happened, but I have no idea what. 'What's going on?' I ask.

The girl touches my locker like it's a precious artefact. 'Years ago,' she says, 'like years and years ago, there was this girl, right?'

'Riiiiight,' I reply.

'Her name was Hillary Randle and she was the head girl: beautiful, popular, clever, totally hot boyfriend who was also smart and destined for the big time.'

'I'm jealous.'

'That's the thing — *everyone* was jealous of her. She had a perfect life.'

'So where is she now?' I ask. 'Prime Minister? Supermodel? Owner of a multimillion-pound company?'

'One day she just disappeared. No one knows where she went or why or if she's alive or dead. The police came and emptied her locker and they said they found a note in it.'

'Suicide?!' I don't like the idea of having the suicide locker.

Goth girl shrugs. 'Don't know. They never found her.'

This is interesting. What happened to Hillary Randle?

'Since then,' the girl grabs my arm to make a dramatic story out of this, 'the school thought it would be too weird to use her locker so they just kept it locked. Now everyone writes down their deepest darkests and slips them through.' She points at the vents at the top. 'Like as a way to stop the same thing that happened to Hillary Randle happening to us.'

'Sooooo,' I say, trying to understand, 'you're telling me that there is a secret on every single piece of paper in here.'

She nods slowly.

'A secret belonging to someone in this school?'

She nods again, then pokes me in the chest. 'And *you* get to read them.'

I take a deep breath. This is quite a lot to take in on a first day.

'If knowledge is power,' she says, 'you've just become the most powerful girl in school!'

Whoa. I can't decide if this is a good thing or absolutely hideous.

Chapter 4

'Sorry, Miss Draper,' says the goth girl as she walks into the classroom just ahead of me.

'Yes, sorry,' I say. 'I'm new and I got lost.'

'Not a problem – Maya, isn't it?' Miss Draper asks. She's my English teacher and she looks really nice. Which is great, as English is my favourite subject and I don't think I could handle anything heavy after the morning I've had. 'You have no such excuse, Zeba,' Miss Draper says to goth girl as she sits down. 'Maya, why don't you take a seat over there next to Luke?'

She points to a space next to the boy in the army jacket with the stubble. He's huge and quite scary. He stares at me and I wish I could sit next to anyone else.

Karmella winks at me as I walk past. Hopefully ditching me wasn't bullying after all, just some initiation ritual, and now they'll let me into their group.

I'm hit by a smell of washing powder as I sit down next to the gigantic Luke.

'Let's get started, shall we?' says Miss Draper. 'Ten points if anyone can name a poet and a poem they've written.'

I stick up my hand really quickly. No one else has stuck up their hand.

'Maya?'

'Robert Frost, "Fire and Ice".' I stand up to recite the poem.

'Some say the world will end in fire,
Some say in ice.
From what I've tasted of desire . . .'

I tail off because everyone is looking at me open-mouthed. I sit back down, feeling like I'm in an aquarium surrounded by goldfish.

'Er,' I finish up, 'I've forgotten the rest.'

Miss Draper chuckles. 'I just asked for the name and title, but that's very good, Maya.'

From the way everyone is smirking at me, it doesn't feel very good.

'Turn to page 118,' says Miss Draper. 'I'd like

you to compare the two poems there, working with the person next to you.'

I turn to the scary boy. 'Hi. I'm Maya,' I say to him. 'Pleased to meet you . . . Luke, isn't it?'

He doesn't say anything and I don't know what to do. This is the first boy I have ever spoken to since . . . since forever, I think. I have no brothers. I've been at a girls' school all my life. The only male I speak to properly is Grandpa, and he's losing his marbles. Saying 'Hi' to the amazingly gorgeous Ben Sands is about as far as I've got with the opposite sex.

I pull the book towards me, turn to the right page and pretend to read the poems. The class starts talking quietly.

Finally he says, 'So, poetry, eh?'

'Yeah,' I say.

'What's so great about poetry?' he asks.

'Poetry?' I repeat. 'Ummm. Do you really want to know?'

'I really want to know,' he says with a nod.

I'm not very familiar with boys, but this boy is especially weird. He has auburn hair that might be red if the light was right. We're both sitting, but I can tell if he was standing he would tower over me by a good foot or more. He's wearing a green army jacket, and it's totally against the school rules to wear jackets in class, but the teachers must be too scared to tell him to take it off. I don't blame them.

'Well,' I say, 'poetry allows us to express ourselves in a way that forces people to think about the meaning. Take Robert Frost, for example: he doesn't use loads of long words, but that doesn't mean his poems are mediocre.'

Luke mouths the word *mediocre* to himself.

I push past it. 'He writes about, like, building a wall or something – and because of . . .' Luke looks at me really strangely. 'What?' I ask.

I am about to pull out my hand mirror and check for make-up malfunctions when he says, 'You know you're weird, don't you?'

But I'm trying so hard! I've always suspected I was weird. It took the girls at St Cecilia's eight years to find this out and mock me for it. How come he's discovered it in five minutes? 'Weird in what way?'

'I dunno,' he says with a shrug. 'You're just weird.'

'You can't accuse a person of being weird,' I say, 'then not tell them how to cure them-selves.'

'I didn't accuse,' he says. 'And I wouldn't want you to cure yourself.'

'Oh.' How am I supposed to respond to that?

'I quite like it,' he says.

'Oh,' I say again. Turns out when it comes to boys I can only manage one syllable at a time or else a deluge of drivel comes out. 'Thanks.'

'You're welcome,' he says. There's a pause as neither of us really knows what to say. Everyone else round the room is pretending to talk poetry but really talking about anything else. I risk a glance over at Karmella, who's throwing her blonde ringlets back and laughing at something the amazingly gorgeous Ben Sands is saying. God, I wish I could be more beautiful and confident like her. Then no one would think I was weird, everyone would think I was cool, no one would pass notes about me in class, and I would never be bullied again.

'You don't want to be like her,' says Luke.

Is this boy a mind reader? 'Why not?'

'She's boring.'

I say nothing. She doesn't look boring to me, she looks like a person who has a life eighty-eight times more interesting than mine.

'But if you did want to be like her, can I give you some advice?'

I whip my head round fast. 'Yes, please, anything!'

Luke laughs. He's caught me out. 'In this school, it helps if you don't care too much about stuff.'

Leaning back in my chair to appear relaxed, I say, 'Oh, right. OK. Tell me more . . . but only if, you know . . . if you want to. I'm not bothered.'

He laughs again. 'If people find out what you really care about, they can use it against you.'

I know all about that already.

'Even the people you think are your mates will take your secrets, twist them up and turn them into daggers to stab you in the back with. So if you have any, keep them to yourself.'

'I don't have any!' I protest, throwing up my hands to show I'm not holding a gun or concealing a sixth finger or anything. 'Mates, or secrets.'

'You seem like a nice girl,' he says, 'but you must have lived long enough to build up a secret or two.'

I gulp. 'I don't know what you're talking about,' I say.

Truth is, he's right. I have a few secrets . . .

'Right. Well. I'm just telling you. As a friend.'

'Thanks.'

I think I just made my first friend in Mount Selwyn.

What's weird is that my first friend appears to be a boy.

Chapter 5

*Can't wait to see you later, Beffs. You won't believe
what's happened!*

Frankie texts right back.

Will be at yours in about an hour x x

Tomorrow is another day and all that. But first
I have to sort out the mess of today; I'm going to
go down to my locker, clean off the graffiti, then
throw all the papers away.

I look around and everywhere is quiet and empty. It's been twenty-five minutes since the bell went
for the end of school and already the place is desert-
ed. I open a few random doors and eventually find
the caretaker's cupboard. I borrow a bucket, sponge,
cleaning stuff and bin-bags and head to locker 62.

When I get there, the goth girl is waiting for
me.

'Hi,' she says, her black-rimmed eyes staring. 'I
didn't introduce myself properly earlier. I'm Manar

Sakina Adiba Khan,' she says, holding out her hand. 'But you can call me Zeba: your local 24/7 goth.' She says the last bit with an Elizabethan flourish and a bow, and I'm now certain that this girl isn't my path to coolness.

'I'm Maya.'

'I know,' she says. 'You made quite an entrance today.'

I cringe. 'Oh god, I fell on my bum in front of that gorgeous boy – Ben Sands. It was hideous, wasn't it?'

'I'm not going to lie to you . . .'

We have a little laugh, and it makes me feel better about the whole thing.

'Have you read any of the secrets?' she asks.

'No,' I tell her, and squeeze the secret about me being '*tragically uncool*' in my hand, not willing to divulge the exact, extreme levels of the hideousness of my first day. 'There are too many.'

'I could help you if you like,' she offers.

'Help me chuck them?'

'Don't do that!' says Zeba, and throws herself forward, grabbing my hand. 'Don't you see what a unique opportunity this is?! We could learn so much about everyone in the school. And that would help us . . .'

She doesn't say it, but I think she's thinking it would help us become popular. It's a good idea.

'OK,' I say. 'We can take them to my house. My best friend Frankie is coming over too. She'll join in.'

'Great!' says Zeba. 'We'll be a force to be reckoned with, like Charlie's Angels or X-Men or something.'

'Whatever you say.'

I pass her the roll of bin bags and we rip off one each. Zeba seems to hold her breath as she waits for me to open the locker. The papers pour out on to the floor and this time I let them.

'Wow!' says Zeba.

I crouch on the floor and start shovelling them into my bag. 'If you're going to help, help.'

Zeba kneels on the floor beside me and starts scooping the secrets into her bag until finally we've got them all packed in. She stands up and pushes the papers down so she can tie the bin bag shut.

Zeba seems so eager to look at the secrets that she might explode. I'll clean off the front of the locker another time.

'Let's go,' I say. 'My flat isn't far.'

We drop the cleaning stuff back into the

cupboard on our way out of the building then we walk out into the playground, each of us with a school bag on our back and carrying a bin bag full of secrets. It's the middle of October but it's not that cold.

'Are you into Valentine Death Pact?' she asks.

A death pact on my first day?! 'I don't think it's come to that, has it?'

'No!' she says, laughs and bashes me with the bin bag. 'They are the most amazing band. A lot of the time I sit in the dark and listen to them on repeat.'

'Oh,' I say. She's weirder than I thought.

'How long have you been in Greenford?' she asks.

'Not long. We've moved back closer to my gran and grandpa. Just while my mum sorts herself out.'

'Well, it's not the best, but there's a Laser Quest that's just opened up on the high street.'

I raise my eyebrows. Laser Quest might be fun, but I'm not sure how it fits into becoming cool and popular.

Zeba looks at me. 'So,' she whispers, 'I saw you in class.'

'I landed on the floor next to you. I was pretty hard to miss.'

'No, in English class,' she says. 'You might not realize it, but your daredevil stunt wasn't the most daring thing you did today.'

'It wasn't?'

'No,' she says, 'you sat next to Lucas Marino.'

'Luke?' I say, thinking back to the stubbly giant I talked poetry with. 'So?'

'Lucas Marino is the school bully!'

'What?!' My heart starts beating like mad. This was supposed to be the start of something new, but instead I'm right back to where I was a month ago: in the firing line. 'But he can't be,' I say. 'He was quite nice to me in class.'

'He must have taken his happy pills today.'

'What do you mean, *happy pills*?'

'They put him on medication to try to control his rage.' Zeba nods seriously as if she's the expert on Rage Medication.

'I bet that's one of those high-school rumours.'

'I'm telling you!' she says, then flicks her head round to make sure no one is listening. 'I've seen him myself, popping pills from a bottle.'

So it *is* true. I gulp. 'What happened?'

'Apparently he was expelled from his last school for beating someone up.'

'No!'

'Yes,' she says as we get to the school gates. 'He put the guy in hospital. For months.'

I can't believe this. Suddenly English is going to become something I dread. I'm going to have to stay on the right side of Lucas Marino. I wonder if Mum will let me move me to another school.

Just then, a Mercedes pulls up and Frankie is sticking her head out of the window. 'Hiya, Maya!' As soon as I hear our silly greeting I relax.

'Hiyeee, Frankieee,' I reply and run over to the car. 'Hi, Mr Lovis,' I say to Frankie's dad.

'Come on,' says Mr Lovis. 'I'm dropping Frankie at yours, so jump in.'

Zeba shifts from one foot to another.

'Is it all right if Zeba comes too, please?' I ask.

'Sure,' says Mr Lovis.

As Zeba and I pile in, there is a look on Frankie's face that says she's not completely happy.

'Frankie, this is Zeba,' I say. 'I've told her all about you.' And Frankie's look is gone.

'Hi,' says Frankie. 'What's in the bin bags?'

I give her a wide, excited grin. 'Wait and see,' I tell her. 'It's so, so great!'

Chapter 6

My room looks like a blizzard has hit it. There are little pieces of paper everywhere. Frankie is on one side of me, wearing a lime green shirt with clashing orange trousers and Zeba is on the other in her red and black uniform and goth accessories, both of them sitting in a snowdrift of secrets.

'This is the most amazing thing I have ever heard,' says Frankie. 'These are the secrets of all the people that have been in your school for the past, what . . . ten, twenty years?'

'Trouble is,' I say, 'how are we going to work out whose secret belongs to who?'

'To *whom*,' says Frankie. She can't help herself. 'I don't know, but we have to try. Look at this one.' She picks up a piece of paper from the pile.

I'm getting a boob job. I have saved up £1286 so far. All I need is another £2000 and a fake ID so they think I am 18 and not 15.

'You can't get a boob job at 15!' says Zeba.

'And you could buy a horse for that amount of money,' says Frankie.

Zeba looks confused so I explain. 'Frankie's got a horse.'

'Sir Toby Belch,' says Frankie.

'From Shakespeare?' asks Zeba. '*Twelfth Night?*'

'I'm impressed,' says Frankie.

I'm glad Frankie and Zeba are getting on, but we've got to focus. 'Come on,' I say. 'It's one down and about seventeen billion to go. How do we do this?'

'We'll need to start some sort of database.' Frankie goes crazy for lists. Her happiest day is when there's an excuse for a spreadsheet. 'It'll have three columns: one with the secret in, one with the name of the person who wrote it, if and when we find it out.'

'What's in the third column?' I ask.

'We'll tick that column when we solve it.'

'*Solve* it?' asks Zeba.

'Fix whatever problem they are having,' I say.

'Exactly,' says Frankie.

I stare at the massive pile of secrets on the floor. 'With great power comes great responsibility. Who said that? Jesus? Oscar Wilde?'

'I'm pretty sure it was Spiderman,' says Zeba. And we all burst out laughing. 'So, we work out whose secret belongs to who . . . m,' she continues, making sure her grammar is perfect for Frankie's sake, 'and we try our best to help them.'

'Yes,' says Frankie. 'And we must only use our powers for good. Agreed?'

Zeba puts her hand out and Frankie and I both grab it and do a three-way shake.

This is going to be a lot of hard work; these secrets go back years. Suddenly I get a brainwave. 'Logically this locker 62 thing started when Hillary Randle ran away. Like, look at this one,' I'm drawn to a yellowing piece of paper that came from the bottom of the locker. 'It says:

I think it was you that gave me this wonderful gift. I'll never get a chance to thank you.

'It's ancient. Zeba, have you got a smartphone?'

'Yup,' she says, and brandishes it.

'Google Hillary Randle and find out when she disappeared.'

'I'm on it,' she says, and salutes.

'Frankie and I will start on the spreadsheet.' I

41

pull my laptop towards me. 'Look, Zeba, Frankie's already salivating at the prospect.'

Zeba looks worried. 'Are you doing *all* the secrets?'

'Yes,' I say. 'How else would we do it?'

She looks uncomfortable. 'Make sure you read every one out loud.'

Why is Zeba acting odd? Then it hits me – there's a chance that one or two of these secrets might be hers. We'll have to be really nice if that ever comes up.

'OK,' I say, 'I'll make sure I tell you every single secret I find.'

Zeba looks relieved and we get to work. I start reading them out and Frankie types them into the computer.

A second later Zeba shouts, 'Got it! I've just found an article about Hillary Randle. It says she ran away thirteen years ago. On 28 May.'

'That's just before your birthday, Maya,' says Frankie.

But I'm too busy concentrating. 'Listen to this one,' I say.

My best friend is such a bitch. Most of the time I hate her.

We all gasp.

'Who would say that about their best friend?' Frankie says.

I continue to read.

I have already snogged Craig Baker behind her back. Just wait until I get him to be my boyfriend.

'I would never ever do that to you, Beffy,' Frankie says to me.

'Neither would I,' says Zeba. She just implied I was her best friend.

Frankie's eyes narrow. 'Beffy is the strongest bond there is.'

'What's a beffy?' says Zeba. Her eyes are even narrower.

'Best Friends Forever. BFF. Beffy,' says Frankie.

I'm feeling a little like a territorial war is breaking out, and I'm the territory.

I ignore them and read another secret.

I didn't do what they think I did, but I'll let them think it. Everyone in this school's going to be afraid of me. Starting with the freaks who are completely uncool. Raphael deserves it.

'Maya,' says Frankie, 'are you OK?'

'Yeah,' says Zeba, 'you've gone paler than me with my make-up on.'

I show them the note.

'Oh, Maya, I'm sorry.' Frankie puts her arm round me.

'Do you think it's that boy in English . . . Luke whatshisname?' I ask Zeba.

Zeba bites her lip. 'It could be.'

I hang my head. According to the person who passed the note about me today I'm a completely uncool freak, so I'm going to be bullied.

'Don't worry, Maya,' says Frankie, wrapping her positivity round me like a blanket. 'It couldn't happen again.'

'What couldn't?' asks Zeba.

I don't want to explain about the teasing, the taunting and the mean stuff those girls did. St Cecilia's was a nightmare. The days they bullied me were awful, but the days they didn't were worse because I was constantly waiting for it. Frankie was my only friend, and there wasn't a lot she could do to help.

Zeba's waiting for me to say something, but fortunately Mum calls up from the front door. 'Maya! I'm home!'

'Hi, Mum!' I shout.

'And I've brought Gran and Grandpa with me!'

It's great that we've moved so close to my grandparents.

'Come and get dinner!'

And we all run downstairs.

Chapter 7

We're all sitting round the kitchen table as Gran and Mum stand at the kitchenette separating the portions of fish and chips so there's some for everyone.

'Hi, Frankie,' says Mum. 'I see we haven't managed to get rid of you then.'

'Not a chance!' says Frankie. Frankie knows my mum almost as well as I do.

'And Maya's picked up another one!' says Zeba, as her way of introducing herself.

Mum tries not to look shocked by Zeba's ghoulish appearance and says, 'Nice to meet you. And you are . . . ?'

'Manar Sakina Adiba Khan, I'm your local 24/7 goth,' she says. 'But you can call me Zeba.'

'What a relief,' says Mum, and from the way Zeba laughs I can tell that Mum has yet another fan.

Gran smiles at me. 'Your Grandpa and I thought we'd bring over your favourite tea, as it was your first day.'

'Fish and chips was my favourite dinner when I was little.' I get up and nudge Gran so she knows I'm teasing her. 'I have much more sophisticated tastes now,' I tell her in my best posh voice.

'Well excuse me, Lady Maya of the Denham Dales,' she says as she hands me two full plates. 'What do you care to eat these days?'

'Beef Wellington is my absolute fave,' I tell her, putting the plates down in front of Zeba and Frankie.

'Who's made you beef Wellington?' she asks as she brings over two more plates for me and Grandpa. She turns back to mum. 'I can't imagine you, who finds buttered toast a challenge, can make beef Wellington.'

'Dave made it,' says Frankie, her big mouth open to shove in a chip. 'It's now my absolute fave too.'

Gran hovers over her chair and looks at me. I know what she's doing; she's trying to work out if I want to say more about Dave. But I don't. I absolutely don't. The only good thing about Dave was his beef Wellington, and he only made it twice.

'Mum . . .' Mum warns Gran and sits down.

Gran sits too and laughs it off. 'Well, in this part of the country, posh grub is fish and chips. If you like we can call it *pommes frites*.'

'*Poisson et frites*,' says Zeba.

I kiss my fingers and throw them at her.

'I did bring desert,' Gran says, 'but unfortunately your grandfather is feeding it to the dog.' She points behind me at Grandpa.

'We don't have a dog,' I remind her.

'Try telling him that!' says Gran with a shrug.

Grandpa's sitting wearing one slipper and one hiking boot. I guess he's having one of his deranged days. Sometimes I wonder if he's putting it on to amuse us. We all pretend to find him quite funny, but I know Mum and Gran are worried about him.

'You can have this dog if you want,' Grandpa says, pointing at an empty cardboard box on the floor. 'He's absolutely useless!'

Zeba and Frankie giggle.

'What's wrong with the dog?' I ask.

Grandpa leans forward and puts his arm around

me, as if he doesn't want the dog to hear what he's about to say. Which is weird for two reasons:

a) the dog is a cardboard box, and

b) even if the cardboard box *was* a dog, he wouldn't be able to understand.

'When I took him to the park he wouldn't play fetch,' he whispers.

'Oh dear,' I say, like I'm a vet and very concerned.

'It used to be Hitachi's favourite game.' Grandpa shakes his head sadly.

'Why is the dog called Hitachi?' Frankie asks.

'It's written down his side.' Grandpa points at the box dog, and it's true. 'Good dog,' I say, and pat the box on the head.

'Leanne,' said Grandpa, looking up at Mum as if he's only just noticed she's there. 'You really need to cut down on all those chocolates. You've put on a lot of weight recently.'

The rest of us look at each other, stunned for a minute. Then we burst out laughing.

'I'm not fat, Dad,' says Mum. 'I'm going to have a baby.'

'What? Another one?!' he asks. Clearly this is news to him even though we talk about it every day. 'But you've only just had a baby!'

'Maya's thirteen, Dad,' she says, shaking her head. 'And she's sitting right next to you.'

Grandpa sticks out his hand towards me. 'Hello, Brian Andrews, nice to meet you.'

Gran has had enough of this lunacy. 'Come on. Eat up.'

'Yum,' says Mum. 'Fish and chips is just what I wanted.'

Gran clears her throat in a way that makes me tense. 'It's no beef Wellington,' she says.

Oh no, here goes.

'Hmmm.' Mum's trying her best not to rise to it.

'I bet it was delicious.'

'I didn't say it was delicious,' I mumble.

'You said it was your favourite,' Gran replies.

'So what?' says Mum, the irritation showing in her voice. 'So he makes a decent meal?'

'I'm just saying that a man who can cook can't be—'

The clank of metal against china makes us all look up from our dinners. I can tell that Zeba and Frankie are feeling even more awkward than I am. 'Because he can cook, you think I should take him back? Never mind that he's a pig. Never mind that he called me a liar. Never mind that he shouted at me in front of my daughter!' Mum's shouting now, completely missing the irony.

'You're carrying his child, Leanne!' says Gran.

It's like a tennis match, with me, Frankie and Zeba looking back and forth at the verbal ball. Suddenly, as if things weren't bad enough, Grandpa starts barking.

'You need the baby's father,' says Gran. 'God forbid, a husband.'

'Bark bark!' shouts Grandpa.

'I don't need a man for anything. And if I did, it wouldn't be a man like Dave!'

I'm with Mum on this one: we definitely don't need Dave around.

'Bark!' says Grandpa. 'Would someone let the dog out?'

'Darling, if you'd just see sense . . .'

I glance at Zeba and Frankie and motion to the door. We all get up and get out of there. Gran and Mum continue arguing and Grandpa continues barking as if they haven't noticed we've gone.

We stand in the hallway and hold our own little meeting. 'Sorry you had to see that,' I say to Zeba. 'Frankie's met them all already, but I guess you had to find out about my bizarre family eventually.'

Zeba grabs her huge backpack and flings it on to her shoulder. 'Your family —' she pauses as she loops her arm in the other strap, 'are awesome!'

And I can tell she means it.

Chapter 8

I've woken up really early for some reason. I think it's because I have a lot on my mind, what with it being the second day at a new school, my mum being pregnant with Dave's child — which means I have to face the fact that she actually had sex with him — Yuck! Not to mention that I think I'm the reason Mum and him broke up.

Frankie's great and everything, but her family is basically normal and she doesn't really understand. Sometime I have secrets I can only tell to my diary.

I reach under my bed and find my pretty notepad with the embroidered flower design on the front.

Maya Andrews: my secret diary. KEEP OUT!

I flip the page and start writing.

> I like living here with just me and mum.
> Even if the flat is tiny compared to the old
> place in Denham and she's never home when
> I get back. Having boys in the school is
> pretty exciting too. Trouble is, I'm stuck
> next to the school bully. But Mum says I
> won't get bullied if I try a little harder
> to be cool. I'm trying really hard, but
> yesterday someone passed a note round

'Morning, sweetheart.' Mum startles me as she opens the door. 'Are you awake?'

I quickly shove my diary underneath my pillow and lie down, pretending to be asleep.

'Time to wake up, Sweet Dream,' she says in a quiet voice.

I groan, turn over and turn my back on her. Mum sits on my bed and strokes my hair. 'I want to say how sorry I am about last night.'

I just mumble because I think there might be more apology to come.

'I was just so knackered after work, and your Gran was winding me up, and I was annoyed about . . . anyway, I'm sorry.'

'It's OK, Mum.' I know it's not her fault. She's always telling me how her pregnancy hormones make her crazy, and I guess it's true.

'It's not OK. I didn't ask about your day, and I had a screaming match in front of your friends.'

I turn around to face her. 'Grandpa was barking like a dog.'

Mum guffaws. 'So tell me: how did it go?'

I shrug and can't really look her in the eye.

'Did you make loads of cool friends? Did you find a boy to have a crush on? Did he instantly fall in love with you?'

One freaky friend and one very gorgeous boy. But I don't say this.

'What's the matter, hun?'

'Oh, I love learning and schoolwork and stuff, Mum, you know I do. But it's the people at Mount Selwyn . . . I really want to be popular, but I'm not sure they like me.'

Mum gives me a big hug. 'Oh, they will, honey, they will.'

'Really?' Mum's always had loads of cool friends, so she must know the truth about this sort of stuff.

'Well, yeah, sure. It just might take a little while because you've started late.'

'But I tried so hard to be friendly and they laughed at me.' I pull at the ribbons on my bed sheets. 'I don't know what to do. I might be an uncool freak forever.' Which means that the bully who wrote the secret will target me first.

'What about that girl yesterday? Zeba, wasn't it?'

'She's OK, but she's a bit . . . strange. I wouldn't say she was part of the cool crowd.'

'You want to be friends with the beautiful girls that all the boys fancy.' Mum sighs. Then she looks me in the eye. 'Want to know the truth?'

'Desperately!' I say.

'You're a super-smart girl, and you are sweet and lovely.'

'OK . . .' Why is she saying it like it's a bad thing?

'But something happens to girls about your age. They become so obsessed with their image that they forget to be nice to each other.'

'They become so obsessed that they ditch me in the toilets?'

Mum looks shocked. 'Is that what happened, Sweet Dream? Did Zeba ditch you in the toilets? Do I need to come in and speak—'

'Not her. The cool girls. The ones I *want* to be

friends with.' The ones that will stop me getting bullied.

Mum frowns and shakes her head. 'They do say that the friends you make in your first term are the ones you spend the rest of your school life trying to lose.'

'Exactly!' Mum's even got stats to back it up. 'And I don't have time to make the wrong friends, lose them, and then make the right ones.'

Mum starts thinking. 'Well, you'll have to find a way to bond with these cool girls somehow. If you need to reinvent your look or take up things that they're interested in, then do it.'

Now it's my turn to start thinking. *Hmmm*, what are these girls interested in?

'Anyway,' Mum continues, and pats the bed, 'you'll be happy to know that Mum and I have made up and there will be no more shouting. Promise.'

'Thanks, Mum.' I pause then ask her, 'So Gran didn't persuade you to get back together with David then?'

She shakes her head seriously. 'Not a chance!'

'Good.'

'Gran doesn't need to know the details,' Mum says, 'but if Dave can't trust me to tell the truth about something as serious as an engagement, then what's the point of having him in our lives? Right?'

I look down at Mum's round belly and say, 'Thing is, he'll always be in our lives now, won't he? Because of the bumpling.'

'We'll see,' she says. 'Maybe he'll be happy to run away from the responsibility.'

Now she's talking about my dad, I know it. I've never met him. I don't even know his name. I asked Mum about him once and she went all weird and muttery so I haven't dared ask her again. Probably some guy at school that didn't want anything to do with me. I'm better off not knowing him. At least, that's what Mum said.

'Anyway,' she says, 'I'll go make you a cup of tea. Two sugars, right?'

'Er, it's no sugars now,' I say. Has been for years.

'Pregnancy brain!' she says, and hits herself on the forehead. Then she leaves the room, shutting the door behind her.

I get up and walk over to the bin bag of secrets. We got through about forty or so last night so there are a lot left to do. I open the bag and pick up a handful from the top.

Every night I turn off my phone and tell everyone there's no reception in my house.

There's no helping this person! Unless I get Zeba to teach them how to love talking as much as she does.

I move on to the next one.

> I fancy Amanda Curran. So much I can't even look at her.

Then he's put his name!

> Mark Nowicki,
> Year 10.

I grab my phone and text Frankie and Zeba.

Zeba texts back.

I know them! Mark Nowicki sometimes does computer club with me. Amanda Curran's in Year 10 and she does cello in the hall every day after school.

Frankie texts: *That secret should be priority numero uno. Don't forget to log it on the spreadsheet!*
Zeba texts: *This is serious business. Time for a plan.*

Let's hope by the end of the week we'll have at least one tick in the solved list. And I'll be the most popular girl in the school for all my good deeds.

Then maybe I'll be able to find the person who passed the note about me being '*tragically uncool*' and convince them otherwise. And then maybe the bully won't target me.

Chapter 9

Making everyone think I'm not tragically uncool is going to be tricky. But getting Amanda Curran and Mark Nowicki together is something I *can* do.

We're standing in the school corridor at break time, surveying the crowds of people until it's safe to put our plan into action.

'What does the note say?' Frankie's voice comes from the phone in my hand.

Zeba takes out the note from her pocket and cups it. There are people walking by everywhere, but the only good thing about being unpopular is that no one takes any notice of us.

Zeba starts whispering to Frankie. 'We tried to copy Mark's handwriting. We wrote:

Dear Amanda,
I am in love with you. I know this might come as some surprise because I never look at you but it's because I love you so much

that I can't look at you. If you would give me a sign that you liked me I would ask you out in a second. Do nothing and neither will I.

With all my hopeful heart,

Mark N x x

I give Zeba a small round of applause. 'Truly an Oscar-winning performance!'

Zeba takes a bow.

'Beautiful and poetic writing with superb delivery, my darlings,' says Frankie. Zeba and I nod at each other with pride. 'But I'm afraid there might be a problem.'

'What?' we say together.

'No one would believe a boy wrote that,' she says.

'Why not?' I ask.

Frankie sighs. 'I have three brothers and I have never heard them say more than five words at a time. If they string two sentences together, they're having a chatty day.'

Zeba and I wince at each other. 'She might have a point,' says Zeba. 'When my brother got married, his speech wasn't as romantic as this.'

'It's got to be believable,' says Frankie. 'I bet you even spelled it correctly!'

'The hearts on the i's were probably overdoing it,' I say with a giggle. 'OK, we'll rewrite.'

Zeba turns away and then looks back at me, panicked. 'Quick, that's Amanda coming down the hall now!'

In the distance I see the girl Zeba is pointing at. She's tall and skinny with mousy hair cut in a bob. She's holding a pile of books close to her chest and a heavy cello in her other hand. She's struggling as she gets jostled by the people bumping past her. I reach into my bag and pull out a sheet of A4 paper (not the pink scented stuff we used before). I rip it in half, risk another look at Amanda, and see we have absolutely no time to do it.

Suddenly fortune steps in, and Amanda lurches forwards and drops all her books and her cello.

I start scrawling.

'What are you writing?' asks Frankie.

'*i fancie u*,' I say, forgetting to whisper.

'Lezzer!' someone shouts as they walk by. We ignore them.

'That can't be enough,' says Zeba.

'It's perfect!' Frankie yells through the phone.

Amanda has picked up her books and her cello and is red-faced as she makes her way down the hall again. I have just enough time to write '*Luv Mark N x*' on the bottom of the note before I slip it in her locker.

Zeba and I stand back and pretend to be on the phone as Amanda approaches.

'It's so romantic,' says Zeba. 'She has absolutely no idea. It's like the Valentine Death Pact song "You Don't Know I Love You Coz I'm Dead". There's a line in it that goes . . .'

But I'm not listening to Zeba. I'm looking over her shoulder at Amanda. She looks really sad as she opens her locker. She's about to stuff her books on the shelf when she notices the piece of paper. Her frown deepens as she balances all her books in one hand and picks it up. She reads it and all of a sudden a huge smile brushes across her face, making her look suddenly pretty.

'Yes!' I shout.

Amanda looks in my direction. I quickly turn to Zeba and say, 'Double maths! My favourite!'

Amanda looks back at the note, then down the corridor left and right. She must be looking for Mark. Of course he's not there. But she grins again, puts her books in her locker and skips down the hall hugging her cello.

'Yes, yes, yes!' Zeba and I do a high five.

'Top work, troops,' says Frankie down the phone. 'I wish I was there to see it.' We hear the bell in Frankie's school. 'You ladies go put stage two into action. I've got to go to geoggers.'

We hang up, promising to text her when the deed is done. Then we head downstairs to the lunch room to find Mark Nowicki.

In front of us I see Luke Marino. 'There's Luke,' I whisper to Zeba. He's towering over some other boy who has ginger hair and freckles. 'He's massive, isn't he?'

'That's because he's fifteen.'

'Fifteen?' I frown at her. 'Then how come he's in our year?'

'Because when he was thrown out of his last school he had missed so much they put him back a year.' She grabs my arm and drags me into the lunch room. 'Look at the way he's talking to Angus McAllister!'

I peer back round the corner and see that Luke has the freckly boy – Angus McAllister – by the collar. He *is* a bully. Which means I'm in deep trouble.

'There he is,' says Zeba. I think she means Luke, but when I look up she's staring at another boy, who's sitting at one of the tables.

'Who?' I ask.

'Hi, Mark,' she says, and she walks towards his table. 'Are you going to computer club tomorrow?'

I guess this is Mark Nowicki. He has short blond hair and he's really tall. He's eating sandwiches with a couple of his mates. He frowns at Zeba as if trying to remember who she is.

'I'm Zeba,' she speaks slowly. 'This is Maya. You and I go to computer club.'

'OK . . .' he says.

'Well, it's not in the computer lab after school tomorrow. It's been moved to the hall.'

'Why would computer club be in the *hall*?'

Good point. There are no computers in the hall. But there has to be some way to get Mark to the hall after school so he can see Amanda when she's practising her cello. 'Er . . . someone important is giving a lecture,' I say.

'Why would I want to go to a *lecture*?' he asks.

Another good point. 'Because it's Bill Gates,' I reply. I'm quite impressed with that lie.

'Yes,' says Zeba, 'and he's giving out money.'

Mark's eyes widen and he grins. 'Cool! I'll definitely be there. Thanks.'

Zeba and I hide our smiles until we get to the back of the lunch room near the French windows. But once we're there we whoop and shout. 'We did it! We did it!' And we give each other a big hug.

'I was Facebook chatting with Craig Baker for *ages* last night,' says a voice next to us. It's Karmella, her blonde hair straightened out today. 'He's so funny!'

Zeba and I hear the words *Craig Baker* and look at each other. Wasn't there a secret mentioning him? What did it say again?

'Cool,' says Rochelle. 'Do you think he'll ask you . . .' She trails off and looks up at us hovering over their table. 'What do you two lesbians want?' she asks.

'Oh.' Zeba laughs. 'We're not lesbians. Not that there's anything wrong—'

'Gary Cohen said he saw you declaring your undying love for each other,' says Rochelle, picking up a cookie and taking a bite.

'He was walking down the hall just now with Ben Sands and they heard you say you fancy her,' Karmella says, pointing to me then Zeba.

Oh no! I can't have Ben Sands thinking I'm

a lesbian! Then he'll never ask me out. 'I'm not gay.'

'Oh,' says Karmella. 'OK.'

'I'm not! In fact, I . . . I . . . I have a boyfriend.' I'm getting good at this lying business. I might take it up professionally.

'Ooo,' says Karmella, smiling at me now. 'What's he like?'

'Well, his name is . . .' I can't think of any name except Ben Sands. 'Hitachi.'

'Hitachi?' says Rochelle.

Karmella is looking me up and down, like she's appraising me. I stand up straight and pout a bit. A fake boyfriend might be a way to bond with these cool girls; like Mum said, it's something they are interested in. But *Hitachi*!? What was I thinking? Still, I have to go with it now. 'Yeah, he's Japanese. Hitachi is Japanese for . . . um . . . Henry.' That sounds good. 'And he's the captain of the rugby team.' Oh, my mouth is still moving. 'And he's in Year 12.' Oh dear.

Zeba looks at me with her jaw hanging open. 'You didn't tell me you have a boyfriend. Did your grandpa name the box dog after him?'

'Er . . . Yeah . . .' I look from Zeba to the cool girls. 'Hitachi went to my old school, and when I

68

moved away it broke my heart.' I look at the floor and give a sniff for dramatic effect. 'It hurts too much to talk about.'

Zeba turns to me and puts a hand on my shoulder. 'That's really sad. I'm sorry.'

I am so sad.

'Yeah, Maya,' says Rochelle. 'Me too.'

Zeba starts squirming and hopping up and down. 'Look, sorry, ladies, but I'm absolutely desperate for a pee-pee,' she says, and it's a little more information than I needed. 'I must have drunk four gallons before school this morning and I've been peeing like a fish without potty training.'

No, *that* was too much information. From the disgusted looks on Karmella and Rochelle's faces, I see they feel the same way. We all watch Zeba leave as she tries to walk and cross her legs at the same time.

Rochelle shakes her head as if trying to shake the image of Zeba from her mind. 'Sorry we ditched you on your first day,' she says. 'It was just a joke, you know?'

I beam, but then hide it as I remember what Luke said about not seeming too bothered about things.

'You're actually quite pretty,' says Karmella.

'Thanks!' I say.

'You could hang out with us, if you wanted,' she says.

I can't believe this is happening. I've got my wish and I'm going to be in the cool crowd. Mum is going to be so pleased. I'm not going to be bullied. Me and Zeba and Frankie are going to have such fun meeting boys and everything.

'Oh wow, that would be—' I start to say.

She cuts me off. 'But not if you continue to hang out with that freaky goth.'

Oh. I like hanging out with Zeba. She's weird, but she's nice. 'I'm not going to ditch Zeba just to be friends with you,' I tell her.

Karmella shrugs. 'OK. Your loss.'

I wonder if I'll regret this.

Chapter 10

'So tell me more about your boyfriend,' says Zeba.

We're hiding near the main corridor after school.

'Not now,' I tell her, trying to fob her off.

'How did you get together? Does he have any friends who are into goth music?'

'Zeba, I . . .' If I tell Zeba the truth, will she tell anyone?

'Shh!' she whispers. Luckily I'm saved by some movement in the distance.

I peek round the corner like a wartime spy. A girl is hurrying back into school. Hurrying as fast as she can while carrying a giant cello case, holding it by the handle and using her other hand to support the neck. As she comes closer I see the mousy hair in a short bob: Amanda Curran.

I duck back and nod at Zeba.

Amanda walks past us and we giggle. Probably not like wartime spies, but this is fun.

'I'll see if I can use my phone to stream it over to Frankie,' says Zeba.

'Good thinking!' I reply.

She gets her phone from her big backpack and I see some clothes and an enormous make-up bag in there. No wonder her backpack is always so big! But why carry so much stuff all the time?

Zeba whispers to me, 'She must be on her way to the hall to practise.'

'And fall in love with Mark Nowicki!'

We both giggle again and start creeping down the corridor after her.

'Do you . . . ?' Zeba asks me.

But she stops and I hear why. It's the noise of loads of people talking.

Zeba and I break into a sprint. We run in the direction that Amanda went. As we catch up with her Amanda turns around.

'Are you coming to see him too?' she asks.

'Him who?' Zeba's face is as scrunched up and confused as I'm sure mine is.

'It's going to be like Christmas in Mount Selwyn today!' says Amanda excitedly. She pushes open the door to the hall and it's packed with students all looking around eagerly.

'So this is where everyone is hiding,' I say.

They all stare at us when we walk in. Then they groan and go back to talking.

I see Karmella standing with Rochelle, and when she sees us she sighs. 'It's just Maya and the goth geek.'

'What's going on?' asks Zeba.

'Didn't you know?' says Amanda. 'I was on my way here to practise cello anyway, but it turns out Bill Gates is visiting. He's handing out free money!'

Oh no! Zeba looks at me and her face falls. I scan the room – there must be over two hundred students. Mark Nowicki is standing with his friends in the furthest corner. 'Our plan has completely backfired,' I whisper to Zeba.

Zeba buries her face in her hands. 'The money was probably a step too far,' she says.

I get out my phone and text Frankie. *The good news: We got Amanda and Mark in the hall together. The bad news: We're with about a million other people!*

She replies. *What happened?*

I'm in the middle of texting her back when someone says to me, 'Is he here yet?'

I look up. Am I dreaming it? I must be hallucinating because the amazingly gorgeous Ben

Sands is actually talking to me. 'What? Who? When?' Oh no, I sound like a quiz-show host with a stutter. 'Santa?' I say.

What an idiot!

But Ben Sands's face lights up and he starts laughing. 'Good one,' he says. 'But Bill Gates is twenty times richer than Santa.'

'Let's hope he's as generous,' I reply, and Ben laughs some more.

'What's your name again?' he asks.

'Maya,' I tell him. 'And you're Ben Sands.' That was a little bit stalker-y. Luckily he doesn't seem to have noticed.

'I don't buy that Bill Gates is coming to the school,' he says.

'Oh yeah?' I give him a cheeky grin. 'Why are you here then?'

'I just came to watch the rest of you fools.' He smiles and gently pushes my shoulder. 'Nah, I don't believe it. But how stupid would I feel if he *did* come and I was the only loser not to get a piece?'

'Pretty stupid,' I say. Wow, I'm talking to Ben Sands and it's going OK. I can see Karmella and Rochelle looking at us. They wave and start walking over.

'Do you know who told everyone he was coming?' he asks.

Yes. Me.

'No idea,' I say.

'I heard it was that goth from our class.' He motions over to Zeba, who's tapping something into her phone. 'She's such a lunatic that she probably thinks Bill Gates speaks to her in her mind.'

'Zeba's kind of . . . um . . . different,' I say, starting phase one of the make-Zeba-cool plan. 'But she's my . . .' I tail off mid-sentence as Zeba climbs the steps and on to the stage.

'Hello!' she shouts. 'Hellooooo, Mount Selwyn, can I have your attention, please?' The students all go quiet and stare at Zeba. 'I've just had a call from Bill's people.'

Ben nudges me. 'See,' he whispers, twirling his finger round his ear, 'completely mad.'

I'm too smitten to correct him.

Zeba yells out to the crowd. 'It appears that his private jet has had a fault. He wishes you all the best and . . .' People start booing and sighing and walking towards the door.

Mark Nowicki walks by me, saying, 'Told you that goth girl was a liar.' And he walks right past Amanda Curran without looking at her.

Our plan has completely failed.

Ben turns to me. 'So, Maya, if you'd got the money, would you have shared it?' He leans forward so his brown curls are almost tickling my nose. 'With me?'

I feel guilty about letting Zeba handle this alone, but this is definite flirting and I can't pass it up. 'Well, I—'

'Hi, Ben.' It's Karmella. 'Hi, Maya.'

'Hi, ladies,' says Ben, turning away from me. The moment's shattered and Karmella has his full attention.

'We're getting out of here, before that nutter —' she motions towards Zeba on the stage — 'locks us all in and starts playing emo music.'

'Good idea,' says Ben. 'You coming, Maya?'

I can't just ditch Zeba. That's not what friends do. 'Sorry, but . . .'

Ben pulls a sad face. 'Does your mum want you home?'

'I . . . No . . .' I look at Zeba on the stage, directing everyone to the doors like a steward from Halloween Airlines. Then I turn back to Ben. 'No. I just have to stay.'

It's the right thing to do.

A text comes through on my phone. It's from

Zeba. *I'm going on stage to get everyone to go home. You look like you're getting close to BS so I thought I'd leave you to it. Good luck x x*

It *was* the right thing to do, to wait for Zeba. But as Ben walks out arm in arm with Karmella and Rochelle, it doesn't feel very good. And I wonder if my chance to be cool has walked out with them.

Chapter 11

On Thursday I'm back in my room again with Frankie and Zeba. Despite the monumental failure with Amanda and Mark, we carry on logging in the secrets. Zeba and I are taking it in turns to read them out while Frankie types them into the spreadsheet. Then we put them into the Hitachi box, which I've covered in pretty wrapping paper.

'OK,' I say. 'This one must be recent because it was right near the top. I'd say, less than a month or two old.' I start to read it out.

I won a poetry competition in a magazine. I haven't told anyone, not even my family. They would think I'm a geek.

'That one's right up your street, Maya,' says Frankie.

'I would be so proud if I won a poetry competition,' I say. 'I would shout it from the rooftop. And never stop. Till I drop. Or go pop.'

They laugh and Zeba gives me a round of applause.

'Words are my tool,' I say with a bow.

Then a brilliant idea enters my head. 'I know! We could hold our own poetry competition. Then this girl would realize that she wasn't the only poet in school and she would become proud of her talents.'

'Great idea, Maya!' says Zeba.

'And it will be really fun to organize!' says Frankie. She gets up and does a little dance. I get on my bed and start jumping up and down. Then Zeba joins me. Finally we're all jumping up and down and whooping like auditionees for *Banshee's Got Talent*.

'Girls?!' It's Mum calling from the kitchen. 'Are you all right?'

We start laughing. 'Fine, Mum!' I call. And then we sit back down again.

'Maya, me and you will ask Miss Draper

tomorrow.' Zeba says, 'I'm going to do something in the style of Valentine Death Pact.'

'*Quelle surprise*,' says Frankie, with a roll of her eyes.

But we can't devote all our time and energy to that. There are other secrets to solve. 'I can't stop thinking about this one.' It's terrified me every day since we first saw it. I wave the secret in front of them, then read it aloud.

I didn't do what they think I did, but I'll let them think it. Everyone in this school's going to be afraid of me. Starting with the freaks who are completely uncool. Raphael deserves it.

'We need to stop this person bullying,' I tell them. 'Find out who wrote this and tell the teachers.'

'And find this Raphael person,' says Frankie. 'Warn him that a bully is out to get him.'

'Do you know anyone called Raphael, Zeba?' I ask.

Zeba closes her eyes as she thinks. 'No. Sorry.'

'Hmmm, cryptic,' says Frankie. 'I'm no psychologist –' Frankie thinks she *is* a psychologist because she reads agony-aunt columns – 'but this bully is obviously a very secretive person. He's not even writing down what it is he didn't do.'

He might be secretive, but that just makes things worse for me; as someone passed a note calling me the most tragically uncool freak on my very first day, I must be target numero uno. Me and this Raphael . . . whoever he is.

Zeba squints. 'Why would anyone say they did something that they didn't?'

'We'll never figure out that one,' says Frankie.

Our conversation is interrupted by the doorbell. Who could that be? Mum doesn't know anyone in Greenford any more.

I hear the front door opening. Then a muffled voice. It's deep. A man's voice. But I can't hear what he's saying.

Then there's a pause and the flat is completely silent.

Then, 'What the hell are *you* doing here?' says Mum. 'How did you find us?'

I can hear the muffled voice more clearly now. It says, 'Don't blame your mum. I've been desperate.'

It's Dave.

I turn to the girls and I can feel that the colour has drained from my face. 'I think you'd better go,' I say.

Chapter 12

Domestic carnage is about to unfold, and if I don't get my friends out asap they'll realize that Grandpa is the most sane member of my family. Frankie's called her dad and he's on his way to pick her up.

'Maybe it would be easier if you got picked up from Zeba's house,' I suggest, thinking that the atom bomb could be due in T-minus any-second-now. 'Would that be OK, Zebes?'

Zeba goes even more flippy than usual and garbles something about *wall paper* and *decorating* and her house not being fit for human consumption.

'*Okaaaaaay*,' says Frankie, who's not as used to Zeba's weirdness as I am.

Zeba grabs her big backpack and runs out of the room, shouting, 'Bye!' as she goes.

I want to stay in my room, but when Frankie's dad rings to say he's five minutes away I know I'm going to have to show myself to the enemy. Frankie and I creep past the kitchen like we did when we were kids sneaking a midnight feast. From behind the closed door I can hear voices, but not what they're saying.

'I hope he's not trying to get her back,' I whisper to Frankie. 'David's such a knob.'

'*Knob?*' Frankie repeats with a shake of her head. 'Such an unladylike word.'

From the kitchen we can hear '*try again*', and '*for the sake of our child*'.

Frankie looks at me. She knows how seriously I take this. I hate Dave. He's not good enough for my mum, and I don't want them to get married. Frankie bites her lip before she says quietly, 'Maybe it wouldn't be so bad if they got back together.'

I shoot her a dirty look and we stop and stare at each other in the hallway.

'At least then you could move back to Denham and everything could be like it was and we could be proper beffies again.'

'We *are* proper beffies!' I say, then curse myself for speaking too loudly.

'No, we're not,' she says, turning the volume up even louder. 'We're text beffies. It's not the same. And now you're speaking all differently, and Zeba's in the picture, and I'm not sure—'

'Maya,' comes a male voice from behind me, 'I thought I heard you. It's so good to see you again!'

Dave. Stinking Dave. Stinking, no shoes in the house, always bumps his head, TV hogging, beef Wellington making, stinking Dave. He's standing there with his arms open as if he thinks I'm going to run over and give him a hug.

I don't.

He turns his gesture into a yawn to try to salvage some dignity.

'And Frankie,' he says. 'Good to see you too. How's the horse? Toby Burp, isn't it?'

Frankie shuffles her feet and corrects him: 'Belch.'

'Not in front of the ladies!' he says, and does his infuriating fake laugh.

'Frankie's just leaving,' I say, and push her towards the door.

Dave doesn't move from where he is, and I can see Frankie's dad's car outside. '*Bon courage*,' says Frankie. It's her way of saying good luck. 'Call me later,' she says, and gives me a hug.

Dave hasn't changed. Oversized Adam's apple? Check. Smelly herbal tea? Check. Desperate cheesy grin? Check. OK, he's cut his hair since I last saw him, but apart from that . . .

'They finally fixed the pothole outside our house,' he says.

'That must make Mr Mayhew very happy,' says Mum.

We're all sitting round the kitchen table drinking tea as if everything's normal with this picture.

'It's getting really dark out there,' I say. 'What time did you say you were leaving, David?'

'Maya!' snaps Mum. 'Apologize to Dave this instant.'

I hang my head.

'It's OK, Maya,' Dave says. He leans forward and tries to look me in the eye. 'I just really need to talk to your mum.' He turns back to her. 'I need to know how the baby is doing. I need to come to the appointments with you.'

'I don't know, Dave.' Mum stares into her lap. 'If we're not going to be together, maybe it's best for the baby if you stay away.'

'Yeah,' I say, backing her up. 'I mean, I never had a dad around and look at me, I'm totally well-adjusted. Normal, some might say.'

Dave rudely ignores me. 'Leanne, I want you

back. You have to take me seriously. You have to take our relationship seriously. For the baby's sake. You're clearly afraid of commitment,' he says, 'but I can show you that——'

Mum's head flicks up at the accusation. 'I am not afraid of commitment!' she says. 'Excuse me for making you wait for a while before I let you move in, but I do have a *daughter* to think of.' She whispers the word *daughter* as if I won't be able to hear her from the next chair.

'So why did you throw away the engagement ring?' he asks, his voice deepening.

We've been here before. I can tell what Mum's about to say before she says it. Something like, '*I did not throw the ring away. I took it off and someone pinched it.*'

'It was stolen, you arse!' she shouts. A new variation on the same theme.

'Leanne, come on——'

'You think I'm a liar!' Mum shouts back. 'You think I chucked it. Or stripped it and sold it for parts.'

She should have sold it. It was huge. Then we could have had a holiday.

Dave stands up, clearly angry. 'If you just told me the truth, stopped keeping secrets, then we could move past this and get on with our lives. I'd even buy you another one. But I can't marry someone who won't own up to what they have done.'

'I am telling you the truth,' shouts Mum, tears in her eyes.

Dave shakes his head like he pities Mum. 'You've lied so much you wouldn't know the truth if it did a naked—'

'Just get out, will you?!' shouts Mum.

Dave looks hurt, but he deserves it.

'David, go!' I order him. 'You're damaging the baby!'

Dave's face falls. He looks like he's about to say something else, but he turns, picks up his silly green leather jacket and walks out. We sit in silence as we hear the front door click shut.

I want to say something to make things all right, but I'm so mad with Dave that I don't know what to say. How dare he say that Mum lies? Mum definitely does not lie. Well, she's not lying about this anyway.

Chapter 13

Luke hasn't said a word to me all lesson, which is totally fine by me. I still have to sit next to him for English, but that doesn't mean I have to talk to him. He's just chomping down power bars and Miss Draper isn't even trying to stop him.

'So,' says Miss Draper, 'I want everyone to pair up again. And your homework is to find three poems on the same theme.'

My heart squeezes. My plan to never speak to Luke again has fallen apart. I look over at Zeba. She looks back at me. Zeba's sat next to Karen Small, who's lovely, but Zeba and I really want to be together on this, and I especially do not want to be with Luke.

I stick up my hand. 'Miss Draper,' I say, 'can we work in threes, please?'

Please say yes. Please say yes. Please say yes.

'No,' she says.

Hideous!

Zeba waves at me and I can see from here that she has painted her nails with red nail varnish shaped to look like drops of blood.

Rochelle lets out a loud sigh of relief. Rochelle and Karmella are sitting next to Billy Beckworth — a scruffy-looking boy with a big stain on his uniform.

'Thank God,' says Karmella. 'We would have had to work with Billy the div.'

'Yeah!' shouts Rochelle, and frowns into her book.

'Maya,' Luke says, his voice low and husky, 'I really—'

Fortunately I am saved by the bell. Literally. I throw my things into my bag as fast as I can, so fast I miss my bag. My pencils go all over the floor.

Luke bends down and joins me picking them up and I'm hit by the smell of clean clothes again.

While I'm kneeling down I catch a glimpse into his open backpack. Floating by his A4 pad is a brown plastic bottle with a printed pharmacy label. It has his name at the top.

'Maya,' he says.

'What?' I say, sounding all squeaky. 'I wasn't looking!'

'Here's my number.' He tries to hand me a piece of paper, but I pretend to be too involved with the pencils to notice. 'You know, for the homework.'

'You don't have to help with the homework,' I say quickly. 'You don't have to help pick up these pencils either.'

'But—'

'I'll do the work and I'll say you did, OK?' I stand up, close my bag and hurry over to where Zeba is waiting.

'You OK?' she asks.

I wait until Luke leaves the room before I answer, eyeing him like a cat eyes a passing dog. 'Yeah,' I say. 'You were right about the happy pills.'

Zeba nods. 'Told you.'

'Come on,' I say, grabbing her. 'Let's talk to Miss Draper; see if she'll help us with the poetry competition.'

Everyone else clears out and Miss Draper doesn't say anything until we're all alone. That's what's so brilliant about Miss Draper – she's sensitive like that.

'Can I help you, girls?' she says, and up close I notice her face is a little lined. 'Is everything OK?'

Zeba rushes forward. 'Everything is awesome, Miss D., just awesome.'

Miss Draper doesn't know how to react to the *Miss D.* thing so she stays silent and waits for us to explain.

I step forward. 'Um, we were thinking . . .' I start.

Miss Draper dips her head and smiles at me. It gives me the courage to continue.

'We were thinking,' I say again, 'of organizing a poetry competition.' I say the last words really quickly so I can take them back if she thinks it's dumb.

'A poetry competition?'

I nod.

'We could call it "Searching for Shakespeare",' says Zeba. This is a new idea and hasn't been approved by me or Frankie.

'We haven't decided what we would call it,' I say. 'But we were thinking it could be an open competition, for all years, about any subject. We could give prizes to the first, second and third places. And even print the top ten in a booklet or something!' This is my idea and hasn't been approved by Zeba or Frankie.

Zeba says, 'Ooo, groovy.'

'Thank you.'

We wait, like she's Simon Cowell about to

make the big life-changing decision. A smile grows on her face. 'An excellent thought, girls.'

Zeba and I give each other a high five. 'Yes!' I shout. 'There would be a panel of judges – like famous writers and professors and stuff – and maybe we could get the winning poem published in a newspaper!'

Miss Draper grins at me. 'You two seem very passionate about this.'

'We'd need your help, miss,' says Zeba.

'I don't know. I'm pretty busy. But if you two come up with a solid plan, I'll see what I can do.'

'Thank you, thank you, thank you,' I say.

'You're a star, Miss D.!' says Zeba.

Zeba and I walk out of the classroom and do our silly handshake. 'Maya,' Miss Draper calls after me. 'I think this is yours.'

She picks up a folded piece of paper and holds it out to me. I run back to take it from her and when I unfold it I see that it's the one Luke tried to give me earlier. He must have slipped it in my bag somehow.

He put his number and then:

Call me if u
evr need to
x

He put a kiss. What does that mean? Maybe it's the pills.

'What's that?' Zeba asks, nodding at the paper in my hand. 'Is it one of the secrets?'

'Nah,' I say. 'It's just some rubbish.'

I shove the note into my bag.

Chapter 14

Mr Holt might as well be talking Martian, for all the sense chemistry makes to me. Still, Zeba and I have managed to find a way to make chemical equations more fun.

'So,' I say to her as we study the periodic table, 'if *Be* is the symbol for Beryllium, *N* is the symbol for Nitrogen, and *S* is the symbol for Sulphur, the chemical formula for *Ben S* is Beryllium Nitrogen Sulphide.'

We giggle like idiots.

Karmella and Rochelle look at us. I stop laughing.

'Zeba and Maya!' shouts Mr Holt from the front of the class. 'Tell me: what is so funny about chemical equations?'

'Nothing, Mr Holt,' says Zeba. 'Sorry.'

'Sorry, sir,' I say. 'There is nothing funny or entertaining about chemistry. Promise.'

Mr Holt looks hurt, like I've just insulted his first-born. He shakes his head. 'I don't know, I expected more of the daughter of Leanne Andrews.'

This instantly gets my back up. Why do I have to carry Mum's reputation round me like chunky costume jewellery?

'And she achieved so much — after her false start.'

Oh God, please don't, Mr Holt, *please*.

'What *are* you talking about, sir?' Karmella asks him.

No. Don't say it. *Please*.

'Maya's mother was your age when she had her. Try to imagine . . .'

But there is no point in him continuing. No one is listening. Even Zeba has turned to stare at me. The room is filled with the noise of thirty people trying to whisper quietly, but all I can hear is my name, on repeat. I bury my head on the desk.

'Calm down, class.' Mr Holt is trying to stop the madness that he caused. 'We should be applauding Maya's mother. She overcame the struggles of her teenage years and became very successful in her field. She should be an inspiration to you all. Not that I'm recommending—'

The bell goes and everyone gets up. Karmella

turns to me. 'Wow, your mum was an early starter,' she says.

Zeba puts her arm round me. 'Come on, Maya, let's get out of here.'

I throw her a weak smile as I start to gather my things up.

'Raising a kid at our age must have been tough.' I don't look up, but from the deep voice and the clean-clothes smell I can tell it's Luke. 'I think your mum is brave.'

That was a really sweet thing to say. I lift my head to say something back, but he's already walking out the door.

Zeba's silence, a phenomenon that has never happened before, shows that she is just as shocked as I am.

'I . . . He . . . Luke . . .' she says.

'I know!' I say. 'I'm not completely fluent in Boysish, but that was weird, yeah?'

Zeba nods. She picks up the rest of my stuff and piles it in my arms and we walk out. But Mr Holt takes the opportunity to say something.

'Maya?'

Oh no, he's going to apologize. I stand holding the door half open so I can make a run for it if I need to.

'Maya, I feel like a fool,' he says. He looks me in the eyes so I look away. 'I shouldn't have——'

'It's fine, sir,' I say. 'I meant to ask, what is the atomic number for——'

But he sees through my ploy and carries on. 'It was stupid of me to bring up your mother.' He's shaking his head and I can see that he really regrets it. 'I only mentioned anything because I am genuinely impressed by what she has achieved.'

I nod in the direction of the hallway. 'I have to go, I'm going to be late.'

'Yes, yes. You go. But I'm sorry if I embarrassed you.'

This is just as embarrassing. Oh no, Karmella and Rochelle are still in the room and this is *worse* than embarrassing.

'Don't know why you are apologizing to her, sir,' says Karmella. 'Daughter of a teen mum? You just gave Maya some street cred!'

Did he?

'Did I?' he asks. 'I don't see——'

Rochelle nods at me as she walks out of the door. 'Maya, Mr Holt just put you on the map.'

I can't help but smile. Rochelle just said I'm on the map!

'Thanks, Mr Holt.' I run out of the room after Karmella and Rochelle. I watch them walk along the corridor, hugging their files in front of them with their backpacks slung over one shoulder. I take my backpack off one of my shoulders and hold my file in front of me, like they do.

'What are you doing?' asks Zeba.

I forgot she was there. 'What?'

'Why are you carrying your bag like that?' She scans me up and down. 'Are you copying Karmella?'

'No!' Yes. 'It's more comfortable.' My treacherous bag falls off my shoulder and I have to hoist it back on.

'Looks it,' says Zeba, raising an eyebrow at me.

I move a little faster to catch up with Karmella and Rochelle. We round the corner and I spot them going into the girls' toilets.

'Why are you walking so fast?' asks Zeba.

'Er, I need the loo.'

'I'll come with you.'

I wave her away. 'It's OK, I'll meet you in French.'

'Oxygen Potassium,' she says.

'Huh?'

'*O. K.* You know. From chemistry.'

'Riiiight.'

'Smell ya later.' She sticks her headphones on and starts wailing a song as she walks down the corridor.

I see some people from the year above grimace as she passes them. I like Zeba and everything, but Karmella has a point: I wish my goth friend was more self-aware sometimes. Now that she's gone I can talk to Karmella properly without Zeba embarrassing me. Deep breath, and I push the door to the girls' toilets.

Karmella and Rochelle turn to see who has walked in, poised in position to do their lipstick.

'Hi, guys, what are you doing in here?'

Karmella looks at me like that's the grossest question she's ever been asked, and considering where we are, she's got a point.

'Do you want, like, the full details?'

I shake my head. Then I laugh, as if Karmella has just said the funniest thing in the world.

Karmella smiles at me. Actually *smiles*. 'Well,' she says, 'aren't you a turn-up for the books?'

'What do you mean?' I ask.

'First you have this long-lost Year 12 boyfriend,' she says. 'And now you have this super-cool mum who's been having sex since she was our age.'

I shrug. Change the subject. 'So what did you get up to with Ben Sands the other night?' I ask.

Karmella drops her lipstick. 'Why?' she says. 'Do you like him?'

'No . . . Yes . . . I mean, I like him, but—'

'You *do* like him!' says Rochelle with a grin.

'Is it that obvious?' But I know that it is from how hot I'm suddenly feeling.

Karmella and Rochelle nod.

'Do you think he knows?' I ask.

Karmella flaps in my direction. 'Ben's used to girls fancying him. I wouldn't worry about it.'

'Do *you* fancy him?' I'm afraid of the answer. Because if Karmella says *yes,* then I know I haven't got a chance.

Karmella laughs like I'm her four-year-old sister. 'Ben Sands? No!' she says. 'He's sweet and everything, but he's not my type. I like sixth-formers. Maybe a Year 11 if he was really fit.'

I feel relieved. 'Anyone in particular?' I ask her.

'I'm biding my time,' she says, flipping her hair. 'Making Craig Baker – he's in Year 13 – wait until I give him my answer. I'm in the treating-him-mean stage of keeping him keen.'

'Whatever,' Rochelle says. 'Forget about Craig Baker – why did you ask if we could work in threes in English today?' she asks me. 'We almost had to work with Billy Beckworth?'

'Yeah, that would have sucked,' says Karmella.

'Can you blame me?' I say. 'I'm paired with Luke Marino!'

Karmella looks shocked as she remembers. 'Oh yeah . . . poor you!'

I nod. I'm frowning like this is upsetting news, but somehow I'm chatting with the two coolest girls in our year, which is great.

'Whoa,' says Karmella. 'You'll be lucky if you survive the month.'

'I know!' I say.

'He broke some kid's leg in his last school,' Karmella tells me. 'The poor kid he beat up never fully recovered and has to stay on permanent painkillers.'

'That's hideo— Er, that's *horrible*.'

'Yeah,' says Rochelle, 'but *we* almost had to pair up with Billy the div! That's so much worse. I mean, Billy Beckworth, is, like, the saddest boy in the whole school.'

'He stinks like gangrenous feet,' says Karmella. Then she bursts out laughing, so I do too.

'I don't know who I feel more sorry for,' I say. 'Me, for sitting next to a psychopath, or you for sitting next to Billy Beckworth, who might murder you with his pong.'

Karmella laughs again, but Rochelle frowns.

'Actually someone must have bought him aftershave,' she says. 'He smells pretty good.'

'Uh-oh,' says Karmella, shaking her head in pity. 'His smell has infected your brain. Next you'll be wearing his bright PVC coats, and you'll walk around with stains all over your clothes.'

'Oh God, no way, never!' Rochelle says, looking disgusted. 'But do you think that if he went on some makeover show, changed his rubbish clothes and did something about his hair sticking up he could—'

'Tell you what Roche . . . elle,' I say. I have an idea that will kill three birds with one stone. 'We could ask Miss Draper if I could swap places with Billy. That way I wouldn't have to sit next to psycho Luke and you wouldn't have to sit next to Billy the div.' (And I could become part of the cool group.)

'Oh, thanks, Maya,' she says, 'but I bet she'd just say no. I'm going to be stuck next to Billy forever. I mean, I'll probably end up marrying him or something.' She pauses and looks at Karmella and me.

Karmella sighs. 'If it ever came to that, you

should do a Hillary Randle and run away.'

'Huh, yeah,' she agrees.

The bell rings for the next lesson and we walk out of the bathroom.

'See you later, Maya,' says Karmella.

'Bye, Maya,' says Rochelle.

'Er, yeah, bye,' I say. We walk our separate ways and I watch them go. I'm so pleased with how that went I can't move for a moment.

The hall clears. Luke Marino is the only person left. He has his back to me as he says, 'Have you done what I told you?'

At first I think he must be talking to me, but then I realize he's got someone shoved up against the wall. His voice is deeper than normal, and even from the other side of the corridor I feel scared. I creep sideways and I see he's standing over the freckly boy – Angus McAllister – pinning him back by his arms.

'I . . . I . . .' Angus is pale and cowering. 'Not yet, Luke, I . . .' He flinches as Luke brings his hand up to hit him.

I can't help myself and I say, 'No!' I didn't mean to say it out loud. I didn't mean to say it at all.

Luke and Angus turn round.

Luke drops Angus's arms and says, 'Maya,' as if

my name just fell out of his mouth. Angus takes the opportunity to run off down the hall.

I stare at Luke and he stares at me.

Then I run too.

Chapter 15

'What do you two know about handwriting analysis?' asks Frankie.

Zeba and I shake our heads as we sit on my bedroom floor in the middle of our Saturday Secret Session.

'We need to compare size of letters,' she says, 'and the gradients of the curves in o's and d's and e's.' Frankie has clearly done her research. I start looking at the pieces of paper on the floor while Frankie continues. 'Of course there are the more distinctive features: using symbols for the dots on i's, excessive slanting, a certain colour of pen, for example.'

I scan my eyes up and down the secrets on the floor, looking for any of these telltale signs. I see one with very unusual writing; slanted to the left at a 45-degree angle. I pick up the secret. 'Listen,' I say, and start to read it out.

> I'm one of the coolest girls in school but I fancy Billy Beckworth, the saddest boy in school.

'Oh, that's interesting!' says Zeba.

'Maybe it's one of those girls, Rochelle or Karmella,' says Frankie.

Zeba guffaws. 'You wouldn't know, Frankie, because you've never seen either of them, but the idea of Rochelle or Karmella fancying Billy is insane. Right, Maya?'

'Right,' I say. 'They only go for older guys.'

Frankie looks a little hurt and examines the sleeve of her baby-blue Pony Club jumper.

'The only thing Billy Beckworth is good at is Laser Quest,' Zeba adds. 'Apparently he's a record holder.'

'Quite an accomplishment, I'm sure,' says Frankie, who doesn't look at all impressed.

But hang on a minute: wasn't Rochelle talking about Billy Beckworth loads in the toilets yesterday? If it's her, I could befriend her and persuade her to go out with him. Or, even better, I could work on upping Billy Beckworth's coolness rating – then

Rochelle will be so grateful she'll want to be my friend.

Something about the handwriting on a secret we looked at a few days ago sticks out.

> My best friend is such a bitch. Most of the time I hate her. I have already snogged Craig Baker behind her back. Just wait until I get him to be my boyfriend.

'Look at the writing,' I point out. 'It's identical.'

The girls lean over and *hmm* in agreement. I put the two secrets side by side on the floor. The handwriting on both has the same 45-degree slant and spikiness.

Zeba gasps. 'She writes her "the"s in exactly the same way!'

'These two secrets are written by the same person,' says Frankie.

I shake my head slowly. 'You know what — I actually think Rochelle did write these. She was going on and on about Billy Beckworth . . . and Karmella can be . . . Karmella is a little . . .'

'Karmella's a bitch,' Zeba finishes for me.

Frankie tuts at the insult, then says, 'We need a plan.'

But my mind is blank. And from the looks on Frankie's and Zeba's faces, their minds are even blanker than mine.

We're taking a coffee break from secrets. Frankie, Zeba and I head into town for a Saturday Starbucks Session. We push open the door and walk in.

In the far corner Karmella, Rochelle, Gary Cohen and Ben Sands are sitting on the comfy sofas.

Frankie follows my gaze and sees Ben Sands. 'Who's the hottie?' she asks.

'He's—'

But she doesn't let me finish. 'I can't whistle, but I can do this: *Arrrrooooooooo!*' She howls like a werewolf at full moon. Everyone in the coffee shop looks at her, and looks at me standing next to her. Everyone including Ben Sands. Who laughs his head off.

Frankie has just made a fool of herself in her baby-blue pony jumper. Zeba is standing next to her in a lacy black top, her eyes plastered with more eyeliner than she can get away with at school and she's even got jet-black lipstick. Then there's me, in my jeans and V-neck. Instantly I drop Frankie's arm. I look normal, I think, but how can I look normal when I choose to hang out with these two? I don't mean to be mean, but Frankie and Zeba are weird! No wonder Karmella wants me to ditch them.

Ben Sands cannot stop laughing and Gary Cohen is almost choking to death. Rochelle has one eyebrow raised, and Karmella is shaking her head in pity.

Oh the shame.

'I'm not sure if I want a coffee,' I whisper.

'I do!' says Zeba. 'If today isn't a hazelnut frappuccino with vanilla syrup kinda day, I don't know what is.'

She drags me over to the queue and I order a latte, Frankie orders a berries and cream frappuccino and Zeba her super-complicated concoction.

The place where we pick up our drinks is dangerously close to Karmella and her group. I wave hello and nod, hoping to leave it at that, but of course Zeba has a different idea.

'Hi, guys,' she says. 'I didn't know you hang out in Starbucks. We'll have to start coming here more often.'

Rochelle shrugs. 'Yeah, it's OK here.'

'But we're not so sure about the clientele. Just recently it's gone way downhill,' says Karmella, staring at Zeba and Frankie.

Frankie looks around, searching for the culprit. 'What? Who?' she asks, clearly not getting Karmella's meaning. Her eyes rest on three older girls sitting by the wall. 'Is it them?' she asks. 'Yes, I suppose they do look kind of low rent, as my mother would say. That pink outfit is hideous!'

Karmella's scowl becomes deeper. 'That's my sister, you cow!'

At least Frankie has the sense to seem embarrassed. 'Oh, I'm sorry. I suppose that look is sort of in vogue at the moment.'

'Totally!' I say, backing her up and complimenting Karmella's sister at the same time. 'Where did she get that shiny fluorescent jacket?'

I can see Gary splutter into his coffee and try to hide it when Karmella says, 'I'll ask her if you like.'

'Thanks, Karm!' I say. 'That would be great!'

'Come to think of it,' says Frankie, 'I think Tracy – the girl who mucks out my horse – has a jacket like that.'

'You have a horse?!' they all ask at exactly the same time.

Frankie and her big mouth.

'Yes, Sir Toby Belch.'

It gets worse.

'Jesus!' says Gary. 'Are you royalty or something?'

Frankie leans forward and whispers, 'Some say that we descend from an illegitimate child of one of Edward VII's many flings. But I think that's just Daddy telling fibs.'

I mentally slap my own forehead. Does Frankie always have to sound so posh? I never noticed it before, but it's obvious now.

Ben looks up at me and I think I might melt in his deep brown eyes. 'So, what have you been up to?'

'On your way to a fox hunt?' asks Gary.

'Buying hats for Ascot?' asks Karmella.

I try to grin as if I'm taking it well, but it's painful to be laughed at like this. It brings back memories of St Cecilia's.

'Ascot isn't until June,' says Frankie. 'We'll do our hat shopping nearer the time. You don't want to be out of season and look like a fool!'

Even Zeba is sniggering a little at this.

'But pony jumpers are always in style,' says Karmella.

'Indeed!' Frankie replies.

I have to rescue Frankie before she embarrasses herself, and me, beyond all return. 'What are you guys doing?'

'We were playing dares,' says Karmella. 'Want to play?'

I can't believe this. Despite Frankie's embarrassing behaviour, Karmella has asked us to hang out with her! Which means I get to spend more time with Ben. I nod, trying to seem less thrilled than I really am.

'Dares! Super!' says Frankie.

'Who's first?' I say.

'The Pony Club werewolf?' says Karmella.

'*Moi?* Mademoiselle la Frankieeee?' says Frankie.

'Yeah,' says Karmella. 'Why don't you go up to my sister over there and ask her where she got her jacket?'

'Easy peasy!' says Frankie.

She seems keen so I join in too. 'And you have to speak in a French accent,' I say.

'Brilliant!' says Ben, and the twinkle in his eye makes me need to sit down. I perch on the armrest of his chair.

'Ask her to muck out your horse,' says Zeba, and we all giggle.

Frankie puts on her serious face. 'Right. Done. What's your sister's name?'

'Weirdly enough, it's Tracy.'

Frankie nods. 'OK, wish me *bon courage*!'

We watch as Frankie walks over there. We're all giggling and I start to relax. This is fun. Frankie's walking strangely, even for her, and I realize that she's in character, becoming a French girl, and she's decided that this is how the French walk.

'I can't wait to see what happens,' I say, and look at Ben.

He smiles back at me. 'Me neither. This should be hilarious.'

Frankie's always up for a challenge. I don't know if I would be so brave. Despite all her crazy ways, Frankie's all right. Maybe I was wrong about her being weird. Maybe she'll actually help me be friends with the cool crowd.

'It's such a coincidence her name is Tracy like the girl at Frankie's stable,' I say to Karmella.

'It will be, if that turns out to be her name,' she replies.

'I thought you said she was your sister.'

'I've never seen that tramp before in my life. I was winding up your posh mate.'

Oh. I watch what's going on at the other side

114

of the coffee shop, a little nervous now. Frankie is overdoing her Frenchness, gesturing with her arms and miming horse riding. I can't quite hear what the older girl's saying, but I'm sure she's telling Frankie to go away, but using rude words to do it.

Karmella laughs.

'Fun-ny,' says Ben.

I laugh nervously, trying to join in but feeling bad for my friend.

The girl stands up. Frankie looks worried. Then she drops the French act, smiles at the girl and points over at Karmella.

'Let's get out of here!' says Karmella, and she runs to the door. Followed swiftly by Rochelle and Gary. Zeba shoots me a look; I shoot one back, not knowing what to do.

'Come on, Maya,' says Ben. He stands, then reaches down and grabs my hand. *My hand!* He pulls me up.

'But—'

'Leggit!' he says. Then he drags me out of Starbucks, still holding my hand, and we run until we are round the corner and way down the street. He's laughing as we go, pulling me along as fast as he can, and I don't think I have ever felt this excited in my life.

We catch up with the others at a bench on a little green round the corner. Zeba is following close behind. Ben is still holding my hand and it's hard to concentrate on anything but the sensation of his skin against mine.

'That was genius,' says Gary.

I look up at Ben. 'Do you think . . . she'll be . . . OK?' I ask, panting.

'She'll be fine,' he says. 'That woman can hardly do anything to her in the middle of Starbucks, can she?'

'I suppose not.' But I'm still not sure. I know I wouldn't have wanted to be left alone with a strange woman I've just insulted.

'She's a bit weird, isn't she?' he adds.

I am about to defend Frankie when I realize that she *is* a bit weird. Didn't I think that about five minutes ago?

'Yeah,' says Karmella, who looks down at Ben's hand holding mine and has to stifle a moment of shock. 'She's so posh and immature.'

'How come you hang round with her?' Rochelle asks.

'She's her beffy,' says Zeba, filling them all in.

Everyone is looking at me. 'What's a beffy?' asks Karmella with a sneer.

'Oh, it's just some silly kids' thing that Frankie still talks about.' I'm trying to avoid Zeba's eye. 'Oh, Frankie's all right really,' I say, desperately backtracking. 'I mean, she's into her horses and stuff, but she's nice.'

'It's not nice to inflict that dress sense on the rest of the world,' says Karmella.

My phone vibrates in my pocket. I bet it's Frankie.

'Well, that's Maya for you,' says Ben. 'She's so caring.'

I blush like a lunatic. Ben just complimented me. He's holding my hand, and now he's complimenting me. I do feel bad about Frankie, but I will make it up to her. And hopefully she'll understand when she hears about my new boyfriend. My new amazingly gorgeous, super-lovely boyfriend.

'Yeah, Maya's all heart,' says Zeba, scowling at me. Her eyes drop to mine and Ben's hands locked together. 'What would Hitachi think of you holding hands with another boy?'

'Hitachi?' asks Ben.

'Hitachi's Maya's boyfriend,' says Rochelle. 'I'm sorry to disappoint you, Benjamin, but Maya's already attached. And if you don't drop her hand soon, he'll probably beat you up.'

Ben grins at me. 'I reckon I can take him,' he says.

Wow, Ben Sands wants to fight for me!

'Could I take him, Maya?' he asks me.

'Maybe,' I say, and giggle. 'You're a bit more muscly than him.' Obviously, Ben could take Hitachi no problem, as Hitachi's not real. But it's the thought that counts.

'Wow, Maya,' says Zeba, shaking her head at me. 'Your loyalty knows no bounds.'

I gulp. She's right. I have betrayed my fictional boyfriend and my lifelong beffy in the space of two seconds. But Ben Sands and the cool group are noticing me and I don't know what to do.

'Hitachi is probably used to it,' says Karmella. 'Maya is probably always cheating on him.'

I drop Ben's hand, in defence of my fake boyfriend. 'What do you mean by that?'

'Well, your mum was a slag. It's not surprising that you have turned out the same way.' She says this with a shrug, like she's just pointing out the obvious, but she's just called my mum a slag!

'That's a bit harsh, Karm——' says Ben.

'Hey,' she replies, her hands up in a surrender pose, 'her mum had Maya when she was *our* age.

She must have been shagging around all over the place.'

This speech is getting me more and more angry. I don't know what happened when my mum had me – if I'm honest I've always been too scared to ask – but I've always sort of assumed that she fell in love with some mean boy who took advantage of her and left her when she got pregnant. But my mum chose to keep me and, like Luke said, that's really, really brave.

'It's not Maya's fault that her mum's a slut,' says Karmella. 'But it looks like it runs in the genes.'

I think I'm going to cry. Partly because sometimes I worry about the same thing. That I don't know my father because my mum doesn't know my father. Because there were too many boys to choose from.

'I'm not a slut,' I say, but quietly, and I wipe away the tears before they fall.

'I'm only saying––'

'Shut up!' I say. Suddenly I realize that Karmella is a cow. Why didn't I see it before? She's been mean to me and mean to Frankie. And I let her, just because I wanted to be cool and hang out with her and her cool friends. 'Do you know what, Karmella? You are a complete bitch!'

Karmella gasps. 'How dare you!'

Behind her I see Gary raise an eyebrow, and Rochelle mouths something like, '*Wow, Maya's got guts.*' And they smile at each other. It turns out that Rochelle doesn't stick up for her friend either. Being cool seems to mean being nasty. If that's the case, I don't want it. And I'll take the consequences.

'I don't give a toss about you lot.'

I turn away, leaving them all in a stunned silence. I hear Ben say to Karmella, 'She's right, you know. That was well out of order.' But I can't make out any more. I am off to find Frankie and beg her for forgiveness.

Chapter 16

I am running across Greenford High Street, tears pouring down my face. I can't believe I've been so stupid. I've been rude to Frankie, the girl who's been my beffy since before I can remember. I ditched her for girls who are horrible, have no loyalty, and have no idea what the word *friend* really means. Rochelle has snogged the boy Karmella fancies. And Karmella would humiliate Rochelle for fancying Billy Beckworth. So how are they best friends? I want to turn back the clock and redo everything I did today.

I get out my phone and call Frankie. It rings twice, then goes to voicemail. Frankie's message is her reciting her own telephone number as if she was a character in a Shakespeare play, and I'm reminded how much I love my crazy beff. 'Frankie!' I shout to the answerphone. 'I'm so, so sorry. Where are you? I'm coming to get you. Call me. Please.'

I run to Starbucks, the scene of my hideous crime, and burst through the doors. Scanning the room, I'm very aware that everyone is staring at the crying girl with the stupid boy haircut who is gasping for breath. I can't see Frankie. I run to the toilets and thump on the door.

No answer.

I thump louder. 'Frankie, are you in there? I'm sorry!'

No answer.

'FRANKIE!' I shout and thump and kick the door at the same time.

A little old lady opens the door and frowns at me. 'Oi! I'm trying to take a—'

I turn and run out of Starbucks and back on to the high street.

Maybe she's at the bus stop, making her way home. I run there as fast as I can. If Frankie gets home before I manage to apologize to her, I know she will never forgive me. I will never forgive myself.

'Maya?' It's not Frankie though, it's a man's voice. 'Maya, is that you?'

Dave. I raise my shoulders and gear myself up to say something mean, but when he says, 'Are you all right?' I collapse into sobs.

He puts his arms around me and I allow it as I have no strength to push him away. He hugs me and I cry into his shoulder. 'What's the matter?'

'Frankie and me . . . we . . . I . . .' Because I'm so ashamed I have to tell someone the truth. Even if it is Dave. 'I was really mean to Frankie just now—'

'I can't believe that,' he says, interrupting me as he always does.

'I was! I was hideous to her, and I want to say sorry but now I can't find her.'

He looks a bit worried. 'Have you tried phoning her mobile?'

'Of course I have! She won't answer.'

'Of course you have.' He looks thoughtful. 'Should we call the police?'

'She's thirteen, David, not three!'

'OK,' he says. 'Well, my car is in the car park. Let's drive round and see if we can spot her.'

I don't want to accept Dave's help, or spend any more time in his company, but Frankie is more important right now. 'OK,' I say. And we head to the car park.

We drive up and down the streets of Greenford. I have my eyes glued to the pavements, scanning them for Frankie, hoping that the older girl didn't beat her up and put her in hospital.

'What if she never wants to talk to me again?' I say, but I'm talking to myself really.

'How long have you two been friends?' asks Dave, sticking his nose in. He takes a right and turns down the road to the library.

'Forever,' I say.

'Well, you can't erase forever with one stupid fight,' he says. For a moment I feel optimistic. Maybe he's right for once. 'With me and your mum it might be more difficult.'

He had to bring it back to Mum!

Suddenly I see Frankie further down the street. 'Stop the car!' I yell, like something out of a movie. Dave pulls over with a squeal of tyres, then grins at me.

I jump out. 'Frankie!'

She turns round. When she realizes it's me, she walks away.

'Frankie, please wait!' I run as fast as I can. Frankie stops and waits for me to catch up, which I would take as a good sign, but the look on her face says otherwise.

'So *now* you want to talk to me,' she says. 'But maybe I don't want to talk to you!'

'Frankie, I'm so sorry for what they did back there,' I say. 'It was mean and I shouldn't have let them do it.' I reach forward and try to take her hands but she pulls them away. 'They all started running and dragged me out with them.' Frankie's eyes are full of tears and it makes me cry again. 'I'm so sorry, Frankie. Please forgive me. You are my bestest beffy, and you always will be.'

Frankie looks at the floor and mumbles, 'It hasn't seemed like that recently.'

'I know, and I'm going to do better.'

'You've got all these new friends and it's like you don't want to be my friend any more.'

'I do! Of course I do!' I take her hands and this time she lets me. 'I just called Karmella a bitch.'

'Really? Because of me?'

'Of course!' I say, though Frankie was just one of the reasons.

'Well, normally I don't approve of rudeness and swearing . . .' Frankie smiles at me.

I jump forward and hug her tightly. So tightly that Frankie lets out a groan, and we giggle. 'OK, try to leave my ribcage intact!'

'Sorry,' I say. Then I pause to make sure she knows I mean it. 'I really am.'

'I knew that Zeba was trying to take you away from me,' she says once I release her.

'Huh?'

'I wouldn't use profanity, but if she forced you to leave Starbucks without me, then I guess the proof of the pudding is in the desertion.'

'I . . . No, Frankie, it wasn't—'

'Get it, *pudding* . . . *dessert*-tion!' she says, and I don't get a chance to correct her. 'Hey, isn't that Dave's car? Maybe he'll give us a lift back to yours and we can make a chocolate speciality.'

Frankie and me have been making chocolate specialities since we were five. We can't get enough of them. We jump back in Dave's car.

'Hi, Dave,' says Frankie. 'What are you doing in this neck of the woods?'

Dave looks embarrassed and I realize that he was in Greenford to stalk Mum. God, I hate him!

'All forgotten?' he asks.

'Is *what* all forgotten?' says Frankie with a wink.

'Glad to hear it,' he says.

When we get to my flat Frankie jumps out and Dave stops me by turning round and saying, 'Maya . . .' before I can do the same.

'Thanks for that, David.' I don't want him to start some in-depth conversation.

'Please call me Dave. Like everyone else does.'

I mutter something in response.

'And I'll be here for you any time,' he says. 'And I mean *any time*. I want you to take my number.' He grabs my phone from my hand, taps his number in and saves it. Which is totally presumptuous. 'I know I'm not your favourite person,' he says, 'and I know I'm not your mum's favourite person either at the moment. Your mum can be a bit flaky sometimes and—'

I can't believe two people have insulted my mum today. I snatch my phone back and get out of the car.

'Bye, David,' I say.

'Give Leanne my love!' he shouts after me.

And instantly I decide to forget his message.

Chapter 17

Miss Draper is making us write poems together. Normally this would be my favourite assignment, but how am I supposed to be creative with a lunatic breathing down my neck?

'OK, how about this,' says Luke, as if he's just a normal human, not the biggest bully this school has ever seen. 'You do the first line, then I'll do the second.'

'Um, OK,' I reply. 'Err, how about something like . . . *The sun is shining in the sky?*'

I'm about to write the line in my book when I notice Luke is frowning. 'Maya, Maya, Maya . . .' He shakes his head at me. '*This poem's no good and I think I know why.*' He has a big grin on his face and it makes me want to grin too, partly because I don't want to anger the beast and partly because he's quite funny.

'Sorry,' I say, with my eyes on the paper.

'Miss Draper said the poems are supposed to be about how we feel about school. When I go to school I don't think about the sun shining in the sky. Do you?'

Things were supposed to be different at Mount Selwyn, but it's only the start of my second week and it's the same as it was at St Cecilia's. I'm still uncool. I'm still in constant danger of being bullied. So no, he's right, sunshine is the last thing on my mind.

'I thought you were all about the metaphors and similes,' he says. 'Try again.'

This time I think really hard. 'OK. How about: *These are the socks I wore yesterday.*'

'A bit gross,' he says, 'but I like it. Write it down.'

I write it neatly in my book.

'Then how about we follow with: *With a hole in the toe, but I wear them anyway?*' he suggests.

'Good!' I clap my hands in a tragically uncool way.

While Luke writes his line under mine I look around at the rest of the class, who clearly aren't enjoying themselves as much as me and Luke are. Karmella and Rochelle look bored, and for a second I'm tempted to look bored too. But then I remember that I don't care what they think. And I'm not bored. This is fun. Am I actually having fun with the school bully?

'OK, next line, your turn,' he says.

I think for a second. 'I've got a good one: *The days are as long as the corridors.*'

Luke nods in appreciation. I write it down.

He thinks, grabs the pen from me and writes.

I turn the book to read what he's written. *'Mr Holt's face shines like parquet floors!'*

I burst out laughing. Karmella looks round at me and I glare right back. I'm sticking by what I said to her on Saturday. If she wants to watch me having fun, then let her watch.

Miss Draper calls over to us. 'Are you two doing your work?'

'Yes, Miss Draper,' I say.

'Fascist!' Luke whispers, loud enough for everyone to hear, and I wonder what's suddenly made him turn nasty.

'Hmm,' she says. 'Work more quietly, please.' Miss Draper's attention turns back to her book.

And Luke's smiling again. Is this guy schizophrenic or something? Maybe it's the happy pills. 'OK, next verse. Now I'll go first and you do the second line.' He thinks for a minute then says,

'*Pretend to be me so I'm not like them.*'

What does that mean? He scrawls the line across the page. I want to ask him about it, but the scariest thing about Luke is that I have no idea what will make him flip.

'Err . . . um . . . L-Luke?' I start.

'Yeah.'

'Oh, nothing,' I say, losing my nerve.

'Say it,' he says.

'No, it's nothing. It's OK,' I say.

He pauses before asking, 'Maya, are you scared of me?'

I stare at the page and mumble a 'No', hoping that's the answer he wants me to give.

He leans his head over to one side and tries to get under mine so he can look me in the eyes. 'Maya,' he says, 'I know you saw me and Angus McAllister the other day . . .'

I shake my head and keep my eyes on the page. 'I don't know what you're talking about.'

He sighs. 'It wasn't what it looked like.'

'I'm sure it wasn't,' I say quickly. 'I didn't really see anything anyway.'

He smiles. 'Good. Because I wouldn't want a square bear like you to snitch.'

He called me a square bear, which is only one

step up from tragically uncool. 'Why do you think I'm a square bear?' I ask.

'It hovers around you like a stink,' he says.

'Thanks very much!' I reply.

He's grinning and I wonder if he thinks being a square bear is a good thing. I don't understand this boy.

'Square bear,' I repeat with a smile. 'Stop showing off your rhyming skills.'

He smiles back. 'So you're not a square bear and you're not going to tell on me?'

I shake my head. 'No, and no,' I say.

'Good, because I don't want to be excluded from yet another school. Not when I'm starting to really like this one.'

I think I'm blushing.

'Right,' he says, 'you try—'

The bell goes for the end of class. Luke pushes back his chair, puts on the scowl he seems to wear for everyone but me, picks up his backpack and walks towards the door.

'Sit down, please, Luke,' says Miss Draper.

Luke continues walking.

'Luke! Come back here now,' says Miss Draper.

But Luke doesn't stop. He walks right out of the room.

Zeba runs over to me and stares after Luke. 'Are you OK?' she says. 'What was that about?'

I shake my head. 'I don't know,' I say.

How can someone who is so nice with me be so horrible to everyone else?

Chapter 18

'So I was looking back over the secrets and I think I've solved one.' I'm lying on my bed, talking to Frankie down the phone, staring at the piece of paper in front of me.

'Ooo, which one? Do tell,' she says.

'It's the one that says, *I didn't do what they think I did, but I'll let them think it. Everyone in this school's going to be afraid of me. Starting with the freaks who are completely uncool. Raphael deserves it.*'

'The cryptic one!' says Frankie, and I know her so well I can just imagine her placing her forefinger on her chin as she thinks. 'Who is it?'

I'm tempted to string it out and make her wait but I can't stand the suspense myself. 'Luke Marino!' I screech.

'Who?' she asks. 'The school bully?'

'That's just it,' I say. 'I'm not sure he is a bully.' I roll over on my back and gaze up at the ceiling as

I run through my own thinking. 'The secret was at the top of the pile, so it's newish. He's so nice when it's just me and him – really sweet, and funny too. I don't think he can be the big bully that we all think he is.'

'But you saw him hit that boy,' Frankie reminds me.

'He didn't actually *hit* the boy; he was just threatening him.'

'Oh, well, that's perfectly all right then,' she says. 'Maya, you don't think—'

'When he says that Raphael deserves it, maybe he means *deserves* in the nice way. I think he lets people think he's a bully to help himself, and Raphael . . . whoever that is.'

'Hmm,' Frankie says. 'Raphael is not a common name, so it should be fairly easy to track him down. But I think it's a bit far-fetched.'

'It's not, I have proof!' I pull my bag over to the bed, get out my English exercise book and find the page where Luke wrote his lines of our poem. 'I'm going to send you two photos, then I'll call you back.'

Using my phone I take a photo of the secret and a photo of the poem, then send them both to Frankie. I wait two minutes for the photos to go through — which feels like *ages* — then call.

'See?!' I say, before even saying hello.

'Hmm, the "*them*" on both is pretty similar, I'll give you that.'

'Luke isn't a bully after all!' I yell. 'That explains why he's so lovely to be around when it's just me and him but why he's hideous to everyone else.'

'It could do,' says Frankie.

'And do you see the line he wrote about having to pretend to be someone he's not. That's clearly what he's doing! He's a nice guy, trying to protect this Raphael person. Now I can't wait for our next English class!'

'There could be another explanation.'

'What?' I ask.

'Maybe he fancies you.'

'Do you think so? No, he can't. Maybe he does. But I doubt it. Why would he like me? Do you think he does?'

'And do you know what else, Maya Louise Andrews?' she says, and I pick up a smile in her voice.

'What?'

'I think you fancy him too!' she says this like

she's a detective who's just outwitted the master criminal.

'Don't be ridiculous!' I say, giggling. 'I do not fancy Lucas Marino.'

'Oh really,' says Frankie. 'But he's nice and funny and you can't wait for your next English class with him.' She puts on my voice as she says all this.

'I can't wait for my next English class because I like English, as you well know.'

'And because you heart Luke Marino!' she gloats.

'I do not heart Luke Marino!' I say. 'I heart Ben Sands.'

'Whatever you say, Beffy.'

'Why would I fancy Luke, who looks like a thug and spends his time terrifying people, when I could fancy Ben Sands, who is gorgeous beyond all measure and is one of the most popular people in school?'

'Who are you trying to convince, Maya?' Frankie says, a little too smugly for my liking. 'Me, or yourself?'

Frankie's thrown doubt on my brilliant theory. Luke probably *is* a bully. And I've seen him bullying with my own eyes. Then why do I have this feeling he's pretending to be someone he's not, like he said in his poem?

But Frankie's crazy if she thinks he fancies me. And even crazier if she thinks I fancy him back!

Chapter 19

Mum comes in from work and drops her bags in a heap on the floor.

'Don't just leave them there for me to trip over!' I say.

'You sound like your gran,' Mum says with a sigh.

'Well . . . she has a point.' I don't mean to be grumpy with Mum, but it's almost nine o'clock and I'm starving.

'How was your day?' she asks, coming over and kissing the top of my head.

I shrug. 'OK.'

'Are you liking it better at Mount Selwyn? Have you made any cool friends yet?'

Images of Zeba – crazy, fun Zeba flash through my mind. My friend, but she's certainly not cool. I see Ben Sands and his chestnut-brown eyes. Weirdly, I also see Luke Marino.

'It's OK.'

'See! I told you that moving was the right thing to do. Away from the bullies at St Cecilia's. And away from You Know Who.'

Suddenly I burst into full on tears. Which surprises me as much as it seems to surprise Mum.

'What's the matter, darling?' Mum asks, wrapping her arms round me.

'Everything's so difficult at Mount Selwyn,' I cry. 'I've tried to make friends with the cool girls and ended up being mean to Frankie. I told the cool girls I have a boyfriend, when I don't, obviously.'

'Oh.'

'And I'm always alone when I get home from school. And—'

'I . . .' Mum takes a step away from me. 'You said you didn't mind being alone for a few hours.'

'Well, I lied! To be nice!' I cover my face with my hands.

Mum pulls me forward again and I mush into her round stomach. 'I'm sorry, Sweet Dream,' she says, and strokes my hair.

I pull back and look up at her, my tears making her blurry. 'To be honest, I'd even prefer to have Dave around. With his rubbish dinners and stinky socks. At least then I wouldn't be by myself.'

Mum's face falls. 'I'm so sorry. I've messed up again.' She sighs. Her eyes are welling and I realize that I've made her cry too.

Now I feel bad. I take a deep breath. 'Sorry, Mum, it's not your fault.'

'You have nothing to feel sorry for, Sweet Dream. I've been really stupid recently, but it's the hormones. Once the baby comes I'll be back to normal. I promise.'

She hugs me again, but I don't feel better. Normal for Mum is still not normal. We used to joke about how I was the adult and she was the child. We've done it for years. She's always been like this, even before the hormones.

It's after ten now and me and Mum are sitting side by side in front of the computer, both of us armed with virgin strawberry daiquiris and bagels. Mum gets Facebook up on the screen.

'OK,' she says, 'what is your boyfriend's name?'

'Hitachi.'

Mum raises an eyebrow.

'Don't ask,' I say with a smile.

Mum laughs. 'OK then!' She types in '*Hitachi*' to the profile set-up page. 'What else?'

I have to remember all the lies I have told about him. 'He's Japanese.'

'Ooo, I like exotic men.' She types away.

'He's in Year 12 and he's the captain of the rugby team,' I tell her.

'I would expect nothing less for my girl!' she says. 'Oh, and let's make him a Sagittarius – they are so sexy!' She adds his date of birth, and *rugby* into interests.

Next we search Google images for a cute picture of a Japanese boy wearing a rugby shirt.

'Perfect,' I say.

'He is perfect,' says Mum. 'But perfect is still not good enough for you.'

'Thanks, Mum,' I say.

'Now all we need to do is press *in a relationship with . . . Maya Andrews.*' She links his page to mine and I quickly confirm that we're in a relationship.

'Hey presto – you have a boyfriend!'

And I realize that my mum can be the best sometimes.

'Oh, look,' Mum says. 'You have a friend request from someone called Lucas Marino.' She peers at the photo. 'He looks nice.'

'I don't know about that,' I say. I saw this friend request before, but I'm not being Facebook friends with him. Everyone says he's the school bully, it's only me who's stupid enough to doubt it.

Mum takes the mouse. 'Just press *not now* then.'

'No!' I yell. Where did that come from?

Mum looks at me out of the corner of her eye. 'What's going on?'

'I just . . . I haven't made up my mind yet,' I tell her.

'OK.' She grins at me and I know she's about to do something awful. She leans back, then quickly lurches forward and presses the button to accept him as a friend.

'Muuuuum!' I wail. My mum is the worst sometimes.

'What? If you're not sure about him, just de-friend him later.'

But I don't want to do that either.

Chapter 20

Me and Zeba are looking over the secrets after school. My room is getting too small for all these pieces of paper.

'It might be easier if we did this at your house,' I say to Zeba. 'Bring the box of secrets there and—'

'But we never have chocolate at my house. You *always* have chocolate,' says Zeba.

She makes a good point.

We look at the secrets and Zeba picks one up and reads it out for me to type into the spreadsheet.

I am such a
freak. I wish I
could be normal
like everyone else.

'Are we sure we haven't had this one before?'

I look back over the list. 'No, we had: *I wish I was normal.* Also one that says: *I wish I was like everyone else.*' I pick up another piece of paper from the floor. 'And this one says: *I am an absolute freak.*'

'Are they written by the same person?'

'I don't think so,' I say. 'They all have different writing.'

While I think about that for a second Zeba makes a *hmm* noise.

I look up. 'What?'

'Nothing,' she says. But subtlety has never been Zeba's strong point.

'Come on, out with it.'

'Is Frankie all right?' she asks.

I cough. 'Yes.' I cough again. I can tell what's coming so I don't ask any more.

'I get the feeling she's angry with me.'

I've been meaning to explain to Frankie that it wasn't Zeba's fault that we left her at Starbucks, but I haven't had the chance.

'Why would you think that?' I ask.

Who am I kidding? I speak to Frankie three times a day. It's not that I haven't had the chance – I'm just a coward.

'She hasn't been replying to my texts,' says Zeba. 'Even the hilarious ones.'

'Hmm,' I say. I've been hoping this will blow over.

'Do . . . Do you think she's jealous of our friendship?'

'What? No!' I say, trying to reassure her. 'Frankie's better than that.'

When I asked Frankie if she wanted to come over tonight, she asked if Zeba was coming. When I said yes, she suddenly said she needed to finish some homework.

'Well, good then,' says Zeba. 'It just feels a bit wrong filling in the spreadsheet without her.'

'Like listening to VDP without you. Come on,' I say, desperate to change the subject, 'back to the secrets.'

I pick one up from the pile.

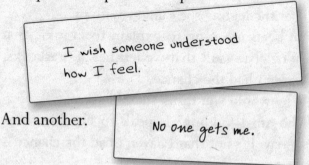

I wish someone understood how I feel.

And another.

No one gets me.

And the next.

> *I wish there was someone
> I could talk to.*

One after another; every one written by a different person, every one saying the same thing. 'They all feel lonely and weird and sad and wish they could tell someone about it,' says Zeba.

'And the saddest thing is that everyone is feeling the same way,' I say. Me included; I'm always wishing I was more like everyone else.

'I don't!' says Zeba, 'but I guess that makes me weird.' She grins. Trust Zeba to be the weirdo who revels in being a weirdo.

'What can we do to help all these people?'

'I don't know,' says Zeba. 'It's so tragically sad.'

Tragically. The word that was used by the person who passed the note about me.

'What did you just say?' I ask her.

'What?'

'Tragically.'

'Yeah,' she says, with a shrug. 'It's so *tragically* sad.'

'Does everyone say that at Mount Selwyn?' I ask.

Zeba starts rifling through the secrets again. 'I suppose,' she says. There are two A4 sheets of paper folded together and Zeba picks them up. 'It's like you and *hideous*; it's just a word we use.'

I try to think whether I've heard anyone else use it.

Zeba unfolds the A4 sheets. 'How many secrets can one person have?' she says, 'OMG!' she squeals, and flips it round to show me.

It's a poem! 'Read it out!'

Zeba stands up, ready to make a dramatic performance of it. Honestly, she could make a dramatic performance out of the back of a cereal packet. She clears her throat. 'It's called, "L Is Hell".'

'L is hell?' I ask.

'Yes,' she says. 'Now don't interrupt.

> *L.*
> *L is heLL.*
> *Neither first to be caLLed*
> *nor best saved tiLL Last*
> *aLways Lost in the middLe.*

If I couLd I wouLd
change my name to Ackerman
or Adams *or* Anderson
waLk up to the podium
and start with a bang.

If I were Zuckerman
or Watters *or* White
the grand finaLe
their Lasting impression
wouLd be me.

They'd say,
'She was good, that Last one,
reaLLy rounded off the show!'

But they'LL never know
cos I'm Lost in the middLe
where L becomes heLL
and Least *and* aLone.
They chose that moment to go
for refreshments.
They've never heard my words.

Zeba puts down the paper and she and I stare at each other in silence for a moment.

'That was really good, wasn't it?' Zeba says finally.

I nod. 'And yet another person who feels sad and unnoticed,' I say.

Zeba picks up the papers again and flips them back and forth. Then she gasps. 'I don't believe it – Maya, look!'

She thrusts the paper in my face. I see the word I least expect. 'Karmella.' I cannot stop staring at the word. 'Karmella can't have written this, can she?'

Zeba is doing a weird mixture of shaking her head and nodding at the same time. 'It doesn't make any sense.'

But there's her name.

'Karmella's last name is Loughton,' she reminds me. 'Begins with an *L*.'

'We need to do this poetry competition,' I say. 'Let's get the plans to Miss Draper asap.'

If everyone knew that we all felt the same way, that we are all as sad and weird as each other, then we'd all be a lot happier, wouldn't we? If a problem shared is a problem halved, what would happen when everyone shares with everyone? So many people would be fixed.

Zeba looks at me and nods. 'That's exactly what I was thinking.'

So Zeba and I get to work.

'Please, Miss Draper!' begs Zeba. 'I swear I will never talk in your class ever again.'

Miss Draper raises an eyebrow. 'Don't make promises you can't keep.'

We're in the classroom, me and Zeba, circling Miss Draper like we're vultures and she's our prey. 'Please, Miss Draper,' I say. 'We'll do all the work and make sure the competition runs smoothly. We just need a teacher so everyone knows it's fair.'

'I don't know,' she says. 'There's so much to organize. Can't you ask someone else?'

'But you're our *favourite* teacher so we came to you.' Zeba's laying it on thick, but Miss Draper's smiling so I think it's working.

Just then, Mr Holt walks into the classroom. 'What's going on in here?' he asks with a cheesy grin.

'These girls have a lovely idea to put on a poetry competition,' says Miss Draper.

'That *is* a lovely idea,' Mr Holt says.

'Let's do it really soon,' I beg her. 'In two weeks' time?'

'Hmm . . .' She might be wavering.

'We promise we'll do everything,' I say.

'Maya and I have designed the posters,' says Zeba. 'And we've planned how the prize-giving will go.'

'I've contacted this local poet called Todd Swift who could be a guest speaker for us.'

Mr Holt and Miss Draper exchange looks.

'If the girls say they'll do all the work and you can take all the credit, why not?' he says with a chuckle. 'In fact, I'll help too!'

Miss Draper laughs. 'Well, if there is another teacher and we can split the workload, maybe I will.'

'Yes!' Zeba and I say together, and give each other our silly handshake.

'Oh, we nearly forgot,' says Zeba. She's looking at me, but I have no idea what she's talking about. 'Can we hold it on a Saturday so our friend can come too? She goes to a different school.'

I'm so glad that the poetry competition is going to give me, Frankie and Zeba something else to work on. It'll fix the bad feeling between us once and for all.

Chapter 21

On Saturday Frankie, Zeba and I stand on the high street. Zeba's in full-on goth mode – black lacy tutu with a purple top, ripped tights and black make-up – only her huge backpack kind of ruins the look. But I'm happy to see that Frankie is just in jeans and a plain blue jumper. No ponies today.

'I still don't get what we're doing here,' says Zeba. 'Are we taking a weekend off the secrets? I mean, I'm all up for a game of Laser Quest – I just like to be kept informed.'

Frankie raises her eyebrows and looks at Zeba like she's a tagalong. 'Oh, didn't you know? Maya and I came up with it last week.'

Through Zeba's thick mask of make-up I can see she's upset. 'Why didn't you tell me?'

'Maya doesn't tell you everything. I bet Maya didn't tell you she fancies Luke Marino.'

'Frankie!' I yell. 'Keep your voice down!' I

check up and down the street to see that there's no one from Mount Selwyn in earshot. 'And I do not fancy Luke. I just wondered if he's protecting Raphael, rather than out to get him.'

'Of course Maya doesn't fancy Luke.' Zeba shakes her head at Frankie and tuts. 'Obviously, Frankie, you have no idea because you've never seen him, but there's just no way.' Then Zeba turns to me with a sweet smile. 'Good thinking about Luke and Raphael. We'll look into it.'

'Look, there's Amanda,' I say, pointing behind Zeba. I can tell from the mousy hair and the tall lankiness.

Frankie tilts her head to the side. 'She's the one who Mark Nowicki fancies?'

I nod. Today we carry out plan B of the Get Mark and Amanda Together scheme. This time we won't mess it up by offering free money.

'Hi, Amanda!' says Zeba, a decibel or thirty too loud. 'How in the devil are you?' Zeba's talking like she's gone mental.

Amanda looks like she's thinking the same thing. 'Er . . . hi . . . um . . .'

'Manar Sakina Adiba Kahn,' she says, her hand outstretched for Amanda to shake. 'Aka Zeba, aka your local 24/7 goth.'

'Riiiiight,' says Amanda, and she slowly shakes Zeba's hand as if it was a pair of discarded underpants. 'Hi, Zeba.'

Frankie stretches out her hand too. 'I'm Frankie, honoured to meet you. I've heard a great deal about you.'

Now Amanda's freaked out. I hang back and simply raise my hand to wave. 'Maya,' I say, the sane filling in my mad-friend sandwich.

'How come you've heard of me?' Amanda asks Frankie.

'A friend of a friend spoke to someone from your school.' Frankie looks to the sky as if thinking hard. 'Mark Nowicki, I think his name was – and he said you were the best cellist he's ever heard.'

OMG. I can't believe what Frankie's just done! She's either a genius or completely blown our plan.

'Mark Nowicki?' Amanda asks, unable to control the smile on her lips. 'Are you sure that was his name?'

Frankie nods. And I realize I should have complete faith in my genius beffy.

'Do you know him?' I ask Amanda.

'Er, no – I mean, he's in some of my classes, but I don't *know* him,' she says, twirling a strand of hair around her fingers. 'Why, do you?'

We all shake our heads a little too quickly. Luckily Zeba's picking up on our cues now. But Amanda doesn't seem to notice anything.

'And he said he liked my playing?' she asks, a huge grin on her face.

This time we all nod a little too quickly. But she doesn't seem to notice that either.

'Wow.' For a moment Amanda is lost in her own happy world. Frankie and me give each other a subtle thumbs-up.

'What is going on?' Zeba hisses with a frown, clearly upset not to be in on the plan. 'Oh.' Her frown turns upside down when someone else walks up the high street.

I turn to see who it is: Mark Nowicki. I pretend to act surprised as I gesture to Mark. 'Oh, what a coincidence!' I say to Amanda. 'Isn't that him? Shall we say hi?'

Amanda has gone a funny colour: pale, then pink, then a little vomity shade of green, then pale again. 'Er . . . I don't know . . . should we? Maybe we should just leave. Or maybe we should go over. I don't know . . . Umm.'

Mark has sensed us looking at him. He looks first at Frankie, who he has never seen before, sees me and tries to work out how he knows me.

Then his eyes fall on Amanda and he takes a deep breath in, looks down, looks up again, tries to smile at Amanda but ends up making a face like someone is pulling a splinter from his finger. Then he does the pale then pink then green trick that Amanda just pulled. It's like some elaborate mating ritual.

'We must talk to him,' I tell her. I remember the advice my mum gave me about Karmella and Rochelle. 'Talk about things he's interested in and find a way to bond.'

'Er . . .' she says.

'But first,' I say, and look at Frankie, 'we need the lipgloss pep talk.'

Frankie grins. 'Of course we do!'

'The what?' asks Amanda, and looks terrified.

Frankie rummages in her bag until she finds her make-up. She pulls out three shades of gloss — pink, plum sparkles and red. 'Pick one.' She offers all three to Amanda.

'I don't know,' says Amanda, who was stressed before but now looks like we're giving her a multiple-choice quiz at the most terrifying moment of her life.

'If in doubt,' says Frankie, 'go with pink.' She points the pink lipgloss at Amanda's lips, and shoots, and scores, making Amanda's lips all shiny and lovely.

I hold up my hand mirror and Amanda does a little involuntary smile. 'See,' I say. 'Now, give yourself the pep talk.' I don't tell her mine – *Cool is everything*. I feel like it belongs to me and Mum.

'Try this,' says Frankie. *'Just be yourself and they will all love you.'*

'Good one,' I tell Frankie, but Amanda isn't so sure. 'Look in this mirror and repeat: *Just be yourself and they will all love you. Just be . . .* Come on, Amanda, it won't work if you don't try.'

'Just be myself and they will all love me,' she says, rolling her eyes.

'Not like that,' I say, and Frankie giggles. 'Do it like you're a cheerleader and this is the cup final.'

'Just be myself and they will all love me,' she says, a little louder, waving her fingers like pompoms.

'It'll have to do,' I say, and I don't give her time to think as I grab her hand and pull her over to Mark.

Mark grins. 'Hi,' he says to Amanda. 'Was it you who sent me this?' He holds up a piece of paper and waves it in the air. It's a flyer for Laser Quest with a note stuck on to the front.

'No,' she says. 'But I got one too.' Amanda looks at me, Frankie and Zeba. I think she has an inkling that this was our idea, but I just shrug and put the next stage of the plan into action.

'How weird,' I say. 'We all got these flyers in our lockers.' They have exactly the same note on the front: *Meet me here at 1 p.m. on Saturday. I want to see you.*

'Who could possibly have sent them?' asks Frankie.

'That *is* weird.' Amanda smiles. 'Especially as you don't even go to our school. Your name is Frankie, isn't it?'

Frankie nods. 'At your service. Maya and I are beffies.'

I see Amanda and Mark's confused faces. '*Beffies*,' I explain. 'It means best friends forever.'

'When one has been *such* good friends for *such* a long time,' Frankie throws Zeba a look that makes me cringe, 'these nicknames just evolve.'

'Well, sometimes,' says Zeba, 'a change is as good as a rest.'

I intervene. 'Let's go inside, shall we?'

We enter Laser Quest and it's like stepping into one of those bad sci-fi shows that Dave watches. There are plastic aliens and laser guns hanging from the walls and ceiling. Along the edges of the room are arcade games and lists of the house rules.

Standing at one of the arcade games is Billy Beckworth. I smile, but then quickly hide it as I am still pretending that it isn't me who set all this up.

Zeba nudges me in the ribs. 'Have you invited Rochelle?' she asks.

'Of course she has, Manar,' Frankie says, using Zeba's real name to annoy her.

We walk over to Billy. He's wearing his bright red PVC jacket (stained) and he's got a load of the Laser Quest staff in a circle around him, mesmerized by his performance. He's holding a blaster in each hand and shooting these little alien things that come on to the screen.

'Excuse me,' I say to one of the staff. He's tall with strawberry-blond hair and looks like he last saw sunshine on the day before they invented computers. His name tag says 'Stanley'.

'This guy blows my mind,' Stanley says. 'He's playing a two-player game, using two blasters, but it's only him.'

'Excuse me, Stanley,' I try again. 'Can you tell us what these flyers are all about?' I know exactly what the flyers are all about, but I have to play along. I push the flyer into his line of vision.

He ducks so he can continue to watch Billy. 'If you get eight people together then you all get to go half price.'

'But there are only five of us,' says Amanda.

Mark counts the group with his finger. 'If Billy plays we've got six.' Billy is still shooting aliens and hasn't looked up, not even when Mark said his name. 'We still need two more.'

'I just saw Rochelle Jenkins from your year,' says Amanda.

Suddenly Billy whips around and both his on-screen avatars get killed as twenty aliens jump all over them. 'Rochelle Jenkins is here?' he says.

'Oh man!' says Stanley, and the other staff members join in the groaning. 'You were just about to beat the high score!'

Billy doesn't seem to care. He might like Rochelle as much as Rochelle likes him. Now that he has been Rochelled out of his computer zone he looks a little surprised to see us. 'How come you're at Laser Quest?' he asks. 'Is Rochelle coming?'

'Did I hear someone mention my name?' Rochelle walks in and looks straight at Billy. 'Are you talking about me behind my back?'

The way they smile at each other is so cute. 'We're only saying good things, Rochelle,' says Billy. 'What else is there to say about you?'

Rochelle melts a little bit and for the first time ever she looks vulnerable and really sweet.

Zeba's mouth falls open. She looks from Rochelle to Billy to me and back at Rochelle again. 'Rochelle,' she whispers, so only me, Frankie and Rochelle can hear, 'are you the person who fancies Billy Beckworth?'

'What?!' she says, her hard face back again. 'No way!' Then she lowers her voice and asks, 'Why? Does someone else fancy him?'

She's sort of given herself away by saying *someone else*, but we don't call her on it.

'What girl wouldn't fancy that guy?' Stanley has been eavesdropping. 'Billy Beckworth is a legend,' he says. 'I am a hot-blooded male, but even I'm in love with him. We're thinking of getting him on TV – he's that good.'

'Really?' says Rochelle. 'So, he's kind of cool then?' she asks.

'Cool?' says Stanley. 'The man is my idol!'

Rochelle abandons us and walks over to Billy and they start chatting.

Zeba and Frankie look at me. 'So it *was* Rochelle

who fancies Billy Beckworth!' says Frankie. She looks at Zeba. 'Didn't you say there was no way it could be her? Shows what you know.'

Zeba looks hurt. She has no idea why Frankie is being so nasty to her. I do, and it's time to sort it out. 'Look, girls, I need to tell you both something. You remember that day we ran out on you at Starbucks—'

'How could I forget?' says Frankie, shooting another dirty look at Zeba.

'It wasn't my fault!' says Zeba.

'You would say that, wouldn't you?'

I am just about to spill all when Mark shouts, 'Can we get this thing started, please? I can't wait to show Amanda how it's done.'

'Maybe it's me who'll be teaching you a trick or two.' Amanda smiles at Mark.

'But there're still only seven of us,' Zeba points out.

'You can go in with seven,' says Stanley. 'Billy is basically two people anyway,' he adds. 'We'll pretend there are eight of you and you can all go half price.'

'Thank you, Stanley!' says Frankie. 'You are a gentleman, sir.'

My heart sinks. I had invited an eighth person,

of course I had. But it's almost half past and Ben Sands hasn't showed.

We are all suited up in our Laser Quest jumpsuits in the pre-game holding bay. On top of the jumpsuits we're wearing our laser packs. If someone shoots our pack, we lose a life. Each of us is holding a gun. Billy has two.

Rochelle ties her scarf round her waist. 'These outfits need a fashion rethink!' she says.

'No, no, no!' says Billy, running over to her. 'You can't wear that – it's bright red! You'll get killed!'

'I wouldn't be caught dead in this!' jokes Rochelle, and smiles at him. 'The fashion police will kill me if the rest of you don't.'

'We can't have that,' says Billy. 'I'll have to protect you.' He grabs her hand and leads her to the game arena.

'Maybe we should work in teams,' says Mark, and looks directly at Amanda. 'It might make it more interesting.'

Amanda stands next to Mark.

Me and Frankie and Zeba smile at each other. The plan to get Mark and Amanda together is working. We've fixed this one. We do our silly handshake.

'That's Team Fixers together then,' says Zeba.

I'm sure the rift between Zeba and Frankie will now be forgotten.

But there is something I *can't* forget. 'Stanley,' I ask, 'will you be able to let us know if another person arrives?' I'm hoping Ben is just running late.

As if reading my mind, Zeba says, 'I don't think he's coming.'

'Who?' I ask as if I don't know what she's talking about.

Zeba says, 'Ben,' just as Frankie says, 'Luke.'

Zeba looks at Frankie as if she is an idiot. 'For the last time, Maya doesn't fancy Luke, she fancies Ben – the cutest guy in school, who she has fancied since the day she arrived! Luke is a bully. Maya has more sense than that!'

'Shows what you know!' Frankie puts her hands on her hips. 'You should have heard the way she was talking about Luke the other day.'

I turn bright red. These two are broadcasting my love life – or lack of one – to the world. 'Shut up!' I hiss. But this only makes them shout louder.

'You haven't even seen Luke, so how would you know?' Zeba says to Frankie, waving her head around as if her neck's gone wobbly.

'I know because I know my best friend. You've only just come on to the scene like a one-hit wonder.'

'Maya would be crazy to fancy Luke. Besides,' adds Zeba, 'what about Hitachi? Why isn't he here?'

'Err . . .' I look around. All eyes are on me, including Rochelle's. 'He's got a rugby match.'

'Who is Hitachi?' says Frankie. 'The box?'

This is it. This is the moment that it all comes out.

Rochelle speaks up. 'Hitachi is Maya's boyfriend,' she says. 'We've seen his Facebook page and everything.' Why does Rochelle have to be here to witness this? I know she'll tell Karmella. I know I shouldn't care what Karmella and Rochelle think, but I do.

'Huh?' says Frankie, being both lost for words and ill-spoken for the first time in her life.

'You would know,' says Zeba. 'He went to your school.'

'Maya was heartbroken to leave,' says Rochelle. 'He was the captain of the rugby team at St Cecilia's.'

'Yeah,' says Amanda. 'Even I've seen his picture. He's hot!'

Frankie looks at me and then looks back at the rest of them. Zeba looks smug because she thinks she knows something Frankie doesn't.

'I don't do Facebook,' says Frankie. 'Don't see the point. But I can tell you that Maya doesn't have a boyfriend. And if she did, he certainly wouldn't have gone to St Cecilia's.'

'What are you talking about, Francesca?' says Zeba.

'Frankie,' I beg, 'please be quiet.'

'St Cecilia's is an all-girls' school.'

Everyone stares at me and I slowly die in front of them. No, that's wishful thinking. Unfortunately I'm still alive.

'Right, are you all ready to go?' asks Stanley, as he opens the door into the dark room beyond. 'Into the arena.'

Chapter 22

In the dim light of the Laser Quest arena I can only just make out the flashing LEDs of Frankie and Zeba in front of me. The room is set up like a maze, with barricades and blocks everywhere. I hear someone somewhere firing their laser and then a girl shriek, and then giggle.

'Wait for me, Billy!' calls Rochelle's voice.

We're walking along in silence, the three of us too stunned to speak. We round a corner and I hold my gun ready. I see a figure in the distance. Then I see the flash of their pack.

Zeba moves forward and shoots. Direct hit! The pack flashes and whirs.

The person turns round. It's Mark Nowicki. 'Shove off, will you?' he says. And I see there is a person behind him. Amanda. Mark turns back and the two of them start snogging.

I want to feel happy about this but I can't.

Frankie puts out her hand for a high five but I push past it.

We get to an intersection, and Frankie goes one way and Zeba another.

'Zebes,' I say, 'I'm coming with you.'

'I don't want you with me,' she says. 'I'd rather go with Frankie.'

'Why?' I ask. 'We should stick together.'

'Exactly,' she replies. 'We *should* stick together, not lie to our friends.'

'I don't want to go with *you*, Zeba,' says Frankie. Then she turns to me. 'And why don't you want to be with me?'

'Because I would probably trip over your big mouth and end up shooting myself!' I say.

'What's that supposed to mean?' she says to me.

'What's that supposed to mean?' Zeba says to Frankie. 'Why wouldn't you want me on your team? I'm a more loyal friend that she is.' Zeba points at me with her gun.

'How dare you?!' I say to Zeba.

But Zeba is still talking to Frankie. 'You are so jealous about you and your *beffy*.' She sneers at the word *beffy*. 'Now I see why: Maya has fidelity issues.'

'What's that supposed to mean?' I say.

'You can't be trusted,' says Zeba.

'Maya can't be trusted?!' says Frankie. 'What about you, Zeba? You're the one who persuaded Maya to abandon me at Starbucks!'

Even in the darkness I can still see the white of Zeba's teeth as her jaw drops. 'Is that what she told you?' She turns to me. 'You are unbelievable!'

I want to shout something back. I want to defend myself, but I take a moment to think about it and realize I can't: I *have* lied. I *have* been disloyal. I have been a rubbish friend.

'Do you know what, Frankie?' says Zeba. 'You don't have to worry that I'll come between you and Maya any more. My first impression was right. From now on, it's every man for herself.'

She shoots me three times in the chest, and my pack whirs and bleeps as Zeba walks off into the darkness.

I turn to Frankie. 'She's right,' I say, approaching her with my arms open. 'I can't really have a go at you for telling them all the truth. I shouldn't have lied—'

Frankie sniffs, and even though I can't make out her face I know she is crying. 'I don't believe it,' she says. 'You told me it was Zeba who made you abandon me, but it was you.'

'I . . .'

'What's happened to you, Maya?' she asks. 'I thought we could survive anything: you going to a different school, new friends coming along, boyfriends, horses – nothing would break our friendship.' She sniffs again and sighs in a way that's holding in a sob. 'But one look from a cooler crowd and you drop me like I was . . . a piece of shit.'

I thought I would never hear Frankie say a four-letter word that wasn't pony.

'Frankie, I'm so, so sorry. Please forgive—'

'See you round, B— See you round, Maya.' She raises her gun, shoots me in the chest and walks away.

I raise my gun, turn it round and shoot myself.

Chapter 23

I'm feeling so sad and all I want is one of my mum's lipgloss pep talks. Actually, I think I need more than lipgloss this time . . . a makeover and a four-hour seminar wouldn't even fix this. My two best friends hate me, and I can't blame them; I hate myself. I've been an idiot, trying to be friends with the cool crowd when I already have the best friends a girl could ask for. *Had* best friends. Now I have no one.

'Mum!'

I push open the door to our flat. 'Mum!?' I run into the kitchen and she's not there. I try her bedroom, but it's empty. I go to the bathroom and it's locked. I knock. 'Mum?'

No response.

I hammer on the door. 'Mummy?'

Nothing.

I phone her. The phone rings in my ear and then I hear it ringing in the room.

'Arrrrrgh.' I hear a moan.

It's Mum! I run back to the bathroom door.

'Maya . . .' She sounds like something out of a scary movie, like she is half asleep or half dead and desperate to get to me. But this is scarier than a scary movie because it's my mum and she's in real pain.

'Mum?' I call. 'Is it the baby, Mum?'

'Arrrrrghowwww!'

I push the door with all my might but it's not budging. She must have locked it, or maybe she's fallen against it.

'Mum, move away from the door!' I shout.

I throw myself at the door. Pain shoots up and down my arm but it doesn't budge.

There is another faint groan from inside.

'Mum, don't worry,' I say. 'I'm calling 999.'

I just hope they're not too late.

By the time we're in the radiography department Mum is looking much better. She's managed to drink a cup of sweet tea, which I bought with the last of my allowance.

Mum has all this goo on her belly and the radiographer is pushing this thing that looks like an electric razor over her bump. She's doing an ultrasound check on the baby.

'There he is,' the woman says.

I've never been to a scan before. Last time, Mum said she wanted it to be just her and Dave. But Dave's not around any more and now it's just her and me . . . and my baby brother.

I've seen photos, but this is completely different. The bumpling actually looks like a baby, and I realize that very soon he will be here.

'Look at him,' says Mum with a deep sigh. 'Is he OK?'

'He looks OK to me,' the woman says with a smile.

'Thank God.' Tears of relief well up in Mum's eyes.

I can see his nose. It's Mum's nose — sweet and upturned and without the bump in it that I must have got from my dad. The baby's clenching his fist and then unclenching it. He's a proper little human.

'In fact,' says the woman, 'he seems very healthy indeed. Second babies often are though.'

'Is that right?' says Mum, with an interested frown. 'Why's that?'

'The mother's body is familiar with the process. It knows what to do this time round.'

Mum frowns harder.

I frown too. 'Are you OK, Mum?' I ask.

She whips round as if she'd forgotten I was there. She smiles at me and nods, tears pouring down her cheeks. 'I'm fine, Sweet Dream,' she says. 'Just fine.'

I'm not convinced.

'Practice contractions sometimes happen at this late stage in the pregnancy,' says the woman, 'but it's nothing to worry about.'

'Sorry,' I say. I overreacted. I wasted everyone's time.

'You did exactly the right thing calling the ambulance,' she tells me. 'You must have been terrified.'

It *was* terrifying, and only now that it's over can I really feel how terrifying it was.

Silence from Mum, who seems a little dazed. It must be the shock of everything. Or maybe the woman is wrong and there is something worse going on. Something she can't pick up on her machine.

'Mum's been working really hard,' I say. 'She commutes from Greenford to Denham every day and she gets home really late.'

The woman turns to Mum and rolls her eyes. 'I don't know whether to be impressed or appalled!' she says. Then she wags her finger at Mum. 'Don't do things that will put strain on the baby. Take it easy. No stress. You should know all this from when you did it the first time round.' The woman looks at me. 'Although I suppose you were a lot younger back then.'

'Yes,' Mum says.

'So the baby is definitely OK?' I ask one more time to be sure.

'He's fine. Listen to that heartbeat.'

There is a whooping rhythm coming from the machine. I know it's a heartbeat because I have seen it on films and stuff; it's definitely beating and it's definitely strong.

'Is that what mine was like, Mum?' I ask.

Mum's still in a daze. 'I don't remember.'

I suppose it *was* thirteen years ago.

The radiographer smiles at me and gives me a wink.

While Mum wipes the goo off her belly and gets her clothes back on, the radiographer comes over to me.

'You're going to have to look after your mum for the next few weeks until the baby comes.'

I nod.

'She seems a little out of it at the moment.' She sighs. 'Is baby's dad not around?'

I shake my head. There's a lump in my throat. Not about Dave — I don't care about Dave — but it's scary being the only one to look after Mum.

Mum waddles over to me. She thanks the radiographer with a weak smile, puts an arm round me and I help her out of the room. This is one of those times when I am the adult and she is the child.

I wish it didn't happen so often.

Chapter 24

School was tough today. I texted Mum about a thousand times and she always texted back to say she was fine. She's stopped working and has agreed, after much begging from me, to rest as much as possible.

The other reason I've texted Mum loads is because I have no one else to text. Normally I'd be texting Frankie and talking to Zeba – or Zeba would be talking to me – but it's *them* I need to talk about: I miss them so much.

It's nearly four thirty on Monday afternoon, and the school is almost empty. I walk towards locker 62. Usually Zeba stands lookout while I empty the locker. But it's just me now so I have to be extra careful that no one sees me.

There's the poster Zeba and I put up for our poetry competition, and a cardboard box underneath for people to put in their entries.

Someone has scrawled the word *Lame!* across the bottom. I suppose I should tell Miss Draper the poetry competition is cancelled.

I peer round the corner. No one.

I open locker 62.

There are about five or six new secrets since we emptied them last week.

'I don't believe it!'

There's someone behind me.

I turn round.

'What the hell . . . ?'

Oh God, it's Karmella. What do I do now? 'Karmella . . .' I start, but I don't know what to say. Her eyes are wide and she simply shakes her head.

I push the locker door to, as if that will make a difference and she will unsee what she just saw.

In her hand she has a piece of paper. She scrunches it up into a ball. 'How did you get that locker open?' she asks.

'I . . . I . . .'

'How?!' she demands. 'That locker has been locked forever.'

'I know, I . . . The school gave it to me.'

'I heard you lied about your boyfriend.' She takes a step towards me, her finger pointing in my face. 'If you're lying to me now—'

'I swear, Karmella!' I say, holding up my hands. 'The school must have made a mistake. I was just given this locker. I had no idea what it all meant. Not until I started reading them, and then—'

She drops her finger. 'You've read them?'

I nod. 'Of course. But I've only used them to try to make people happy. I thought that if I helped people with their problems I could—'

'What do they say?' she asks, a smile slowly growing on her face.

That stops me in my tracks for a second. 'Umm, well . . . they say all sorts of things.'

'Like what?' she asks, smiling broadly now. 'Anything juicy?'

'Well, yeah.' She looks like the locker has put a spell on her. 'I found this secret that I think is from Luke Marino. I'm not sure, but I think he's pretending to be something he's not. Because of someone called Raphael.'

'Is Luke Marino gay?' asks Karmella, beaming.

'No!' I blurt out. 'I don't know.'

'What else? Where are they? I want to see them.' I try to block her path, but she pushes me out of the way. She flings open the locker. It's just the five secrets that were there earlier. She picks them up and reads each one in turn. She gasps as she reads.

'Someone ran over their sister's cat and let everyone think it had got lost! Do you think that's James Steinhardt in Year 12? He's got a car and I overheard him talking about a missing cat.'

I don't answer. She picks up another one, reads it and laughs. 'Oh my God, Cassandra Myles doesn't wear knickers!' She picks up another. '*I wish I was adopted*,' she says in a whiny voice. 'Oh boohoo!'

I grab the secrets out of her hand.

She looks at me and her eyes are sparkling. 'This is brilliant! Where are the rest of them? I want to see more.'

My mind races. I feel protective of the secrets. This is not the response that Zeba or Frankie had. We never laughed or made fun of people's feelings. I slam the locker shut so she can't get back in.

'What's the combination?' she says.

'I'm not telling you,' I tell her.

She steps forward and I have to reverse so my back slams into the locker. The metallic thud reverberates through the room.

'Give me the secrets,' she growls.

'No,' I say.

I say nothing and close my eyes tight, wondering

if she's going to hit me. I wait for ages but nothing happens. When I dare to open my eyes I see that she has taken a step back; she's thinking.

'This is silly, Maya,' she says, a glint in her eye. 'We should be friends — we're *already* friends.'

'Are we?' I'm not convinced by her sucking up. 'You said I couldn't be your friend unless I stopped hanging out with Zeba.'

'Rochelle told me that you aren't friends with Zeba any more. That you and the goth and Little Miss Pony Club had a falling-out.'

'I . . .' There's nothing I can say because it's completely true.

'Well then, what's the problem?' she says, smiling sweetly. 'I'll be your friend,' she continues. 'I'll make you cool. I will even help you to get Ben Sands, if you like.'

My head flicks up automatically at Ben's name.

'I thought you might like the sound of that,' she says, winking at me.

I nod and smile at her. I can't help myself. The idea of being Ben Sands's girlfriend is just too appealing.

She steps forward and links her arm through mine. 'So, you'll be my friend and I'll be yours.'

I pause, but there's nothing to think about. I have

no friends, and Karmella is offering me everything I could ever want: Ben Sands, the chance to be in the cool crowd, and safety from the bullies. She's offering her friendship too.

'Friends share secrets with each other,' she says as she leads me towards the door.

I'm not sure that real friendships are made this way, but what choice do I have?

'Come on,' she tugs me along. 'It'll be fun!'

Whatever happens, Karmella is going to change everything.

'Yeah,' I say, 'it'll be great.' But I say it without a smile on my face.

Chapter 25

As soon as we get inside my room, Karmella is already opening cupboards and drawers. 'Where are they?' she says. She pulls out my pretty notepad with the embroidered flower design from under my bed and opens it. 'Is this them?'

'No!' I shout, and snatch the book from her. 'That's my diary! And you can't read it.'

'Oh,' she says, then giggles. 'Sorry.'

I get out the box of secrets from the bottom of my wardrobe. 'Here they are.' I push it towards Karmella, who kneels before it like it holds treasure.

'This is amazing.' She opens the lid and actually strokes the pile of papers. 'There are so many!' Karmella lifts the box and she's about to tip all the secrets out.

'Stop!' I rush forward to stop her. 'We're trying to keep them in order. The deeper in the locker, the older the secret. Like in palaeontology.'

Karmella looks blank.

'Let me show you.' I pull over my laptop, where I have the master copy of the Secrets Spreadsheet. 'Some of them even had dates written on them, which really helped. But others—'

'Whatever,' she says, and grabs the laptop from me, clearly not interested in efficiency. 'Just get to the good bit.'

'Look, here's one from Mark Nowicki: I fancy Amanda Curran. So much I can't even look at her.'

'That cello loser,' says Karmella. 'Mark Nowicki doesn't fancy her.'

'That's what you think,' I say. 'He put his name on it. And last time I saw them they were snogging each other's faces off.'

'I don't believe you,' she said.

I get the secrets I took from Karmella an hour ago and flip through them. 'Look,' I say, 'this was in the locker today.'

> I had my first kiss with Amanda at Laser Quest.

I throw Karmella a look that says *See!*

It was pretty great, even though it was a bit sloppy.

Karmella is hooked on my every word. I continue reading.

I feel like I can tell her anything — I told her that I shave my nipple hair. And she didn't laugh at me.

Mark's name is at the bottom again. I show it to Karmella.

'He has nipple hair? Gross!'

'Told you,' I say. 'Amanda and Mark are going out.'

'Amanda the flat-chested freak is going out with Mark the semi-hottie?' She thinks about this for a minute, her face showing something between shock and disgust. 'We should break them up.'

'Why?'

'Because it's funny!' she says. 'I bet I could

have him. Even *you* could have him, if you showed a bit of interest.'

'Do you think?' I ask.

'Honey,' she says, 'once people know you are hanging out with me and Roche, you can get anything you want. You can get any boy you want. Just you wait and see.'

I love the idea of being one of the most popular girls in school, but I can't believe it'll be this easy. 'Do you think Roche will let me hang out with you two?'

'She will,' says Karmella, 'if I tell her to.'

Karmella picks up her phone and shows it to me. 'See, three missed calls. Rochelle can't function without me.'

She starts tapping away at her phone. 'There,' she says, and presses *send*.

'What did you write?'

'I told her I was at your house and I'd give her a call later.'

'You don't think she'll get jealous,' I say, remembering what happened with me and Frankie and Zeba and not wanting another three's-a-crowd situation.

Karmella looks at me with pity. 'Not to be rude, Maya, but you have a long way to go to replace Rochelle. She is a lot cooler than you.'

Ouch.

'You think Rochelle is cooler than me?' I say. Then I grab the laptop from her and scroll down to the secret I'm looking for. 'Wait till you hear this: I'm one of the coolest girls in school but I fancy Billy Beckworth, the saddest boy in school.'

'So what?' she says.

'Rochelle wrote that,' I say.

'No way,' says Karmella, shaking her head.

'She did,' I say. 'Remember how she was going on about him in the toilets? Remember how she didn't want to switch places so that she didn't have to sit next to him?'

She shakes her head in disbelief. 'No . . .' Now it's Karmella's turn to be shocked. She puts her hand over her mouth and starts laughing. And laughing and laughing and laughing.

'This is brilliant!' she says. 'I'm going to give her hell.'

I love seeing Karmella smile at me. OK, I'm not exactly enjoying myself, but Karmella is enjoying herself and that means I'm in with the cool crowd. If Mum's right, and cool is everything, the happiness is sure to follow.

'Don't give her hell,' I say, thinking about how

cute Billy and Rochelle looked together. 'I think it's sweet.'

'Whatevs. Show me more,' she says. She pulls over the box and we both start picking them out and reading them at random.

> I stole a packet of condoms.'

'Slut!' says Karmella.

'You need to type it into the spreadsheet,' I tell her, and point to the laptop.

She shakes her head. 'I'm not doing that,' she says. 'I just want to find the ones we can use against people.'

My heart sinks. I've lost control of this.

She picks one up and reads:

> My doctor says I am fat enough to qualify for a gastric band.

'I bet I know who that is,' she says. 'That huge girl in Year 8. She's hideous,' Karmella winks at me, 'as you would say.'

I wouldn't say that. I would never insult someone because of their weight. 'Karm, when I started this I made a promise that I would only use the secrets—'

She gasps as she reads another one. 'Oh my God. It's one from your weird goth friend!'

'She's not my friend any more,' I whisper, missing her now more than ever.

'Look, it says:

> I wear all this goth makeup at school because Valentine Death Pact wear it. But my parents are really strict so I have to take it off every day before I go home.

'That's her, isn't it?'

I don't believe it. It *is* her! I thought that Zeba was a 24/7 goth, like she always says. No wonder she never let me go to her house. No wonder I've never met her parents. No wonder she has a gigantic backpack with spare clothes and make-up in it.

'We should totally get her in trouble,' she says. 'That would be so funny.'

'We can't—'

'Why not?' Karmella shrugs. 'You said she's not your friend any more.'

I think about that for a second. Zeba's not my friend, but I wouldn't do anything so mean—

My thoughts are interrupted by a gasp from Karmella. 'Oh my God,' she says, 'here's another one from Rochelle. I would recognize that babyish writing anywhere.'

'What does it say?' I ask, leaning over Karmella's shoulder so I can read it for myself.

Karmella's gone quiet, and as soon as I see the paper I know why. It's one of the first secrets we found.

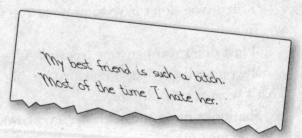

My best friend is such a bitch.
Most of the time I hate her.

I look up at Karmella, who's pursed her lips.

I have already snogged Craig Baker behind her back. Just wait until I get him to be my boyfriend.

Karmella's mouth starts to tremble. 'That nasty little . . .' she starts, but can't finish the sentence.

I put my arm around her. 'I'm so sorry, Karm.'

Karmella falls forward and she can't look at me. She doesn't say a word.

'Are you OK?' I ask her. 'I know how much you like him—'

Her head snaps up and she glares at me. 'I do not like him!' she says. 'I mean, he's all-right-looking . . . but he's nothing special. She's welcome to him.'

'Karm, you don't have to pretend you're OK if you're not.'

'I just don't want anyone to think—'

'I won't tell anyone,' I reassure her. 'I promise. That's what friends are for.'

She looks up at me with her eyebrows raised. 'Do you mean that?'

I nod.

'Thanks,' she says. 'And sorry for saying you're not as cool as Rochelle. Rochelle is a cow.'

I give her shoulder a quick squeeze.

'Let me do something for you.' She grabs her phone from where it's been lying on the floor and taps it a few times. I notice that the tears are completely gone. 'Be quiet,' she says. 'Pretend you're not here.'

I hear the phone ringing. Then a muffled voice picks it up. 'Oh, hi, Ben. How are you?' says Karmella.

She gives me a thumbs up and my heart starts to race. It's Ben Sands!

'Oh, you know, not much . . .' He mumbles a reply I can't hear. 'Do you know who I was hanging out with earlier?' she says. 'That new girl, really cute-looking . . . Yes, Maya Andrews . . . Oh, well, *I* think she's gorgeous . . . No, the bump in her nose is kinda sweet!' Karmella looks up at me. 'We had a great time . . . She's a laugh . . . and her clothes are awesome . . .' He says something and Karmella nods. I wish I could hear what he was saying. 'I reckon that you and Maya would make such a great couple . . .' I smile in delight and give Karmella a thumbs up back. 'Yes, she's single now, I think . . .'

'I'm single! I'm single!' I mouth at her.

'But I doubt she will be for long. I know that Mark Nowicki is interested in her. And some other guy in Year 11 asked her out . . . She said she'd think about it . . .'

I fall back on to my bed in a swoon. Karmella is the best friend a girl could ask for. I zone out as she moves on to a different topic, making the phone call sound really natural. I go off into a daydream imagining kissing Ben Sands and how amazing that would be.

I roll over and idly sift my hand through the box and pull out some secrets from the very bottom. I'm not really looking at them, thinking instead about my beautiful new life with Ben and Karmella and Rochelle and Gary Cohen, all of us hanging out at Starbucks and having fun. But then something on one of the secrets catches my eye. Did I just see the word *Maya*?

I pick it up. It says:

I used to be a geek and no one knew who I was. Now I have your baby everyone knows who I am. I've called her Maya because for so long I thought she was just an illusion, a sweet dream. She's my dream come true.

Oh my God! Did my mum write this when she was at Mount Selwyn? She must have done – she calls me her sweet dream all the time. My mum was a geek like me! Maybe we have something in common after all. Was this a note to my dad that she put in the locker?

Then I remember a secret that we found on the first day.

> I think it was you that gave me this wonderful gift. I'll never get a chance to thank you.

I rummage through the secrets until I find it. I can't believe I didn't recognize the handwriting before – I've known it all my life. This is from my mum. She *thinks* it was him that gave him the gift . . . does that mean she doesn't know who made her pregnant?

A giggle from Karmella breaks into my thoughts. She's still on the phone with Ben so I shove the note under my bed before she sees it.

'Yeah, I'll find out if she wants to meet up with you,' she says to him. 'Don't hold your breath though.'

She puts down the phone and grins at me. 'There you go, Maya – one hot man delivered direct to your door.'

I smile back, but my head is spinning.

Chapter 26

I feel like royalty.

Karmella and Rochelle and me are eating our lunch in the lunch room and I'm sitting at their table. With them. It's weird because it's the nicest table in the dining room, in the corner where there is loads of light coming in from the French windows, but no one sits here because everyone knows it belongs to them . . . I mean, us.

I've only been friends with them for two days and I've had twenty new friend requests on Facebook and been invited to three parties. When I told my mum she was so proud!

Rochelle clears her throat. 'I tried to call you last night, Karm.'

'I was round at Maya's.'

'Oh.' Rochelle looks hurt. 'Why didn't you call me?'

'What are you? The fun police?' she says,

rolling her eyes. 'Look,' says Karmella, pointing to something behind me. She's obviously still mad with Rochelle for kissing Craig Baker. This is a bit awkward. 'There's Ben.'

'What? Where?' I turn around. I see Ben Sands in all his beautiful, curly-headed glory. He looks so much yummier than the salad I got for lunch.

He sees us looking and waves.

I duck my head down and giggle. 'Karms! Did you have to make it so obvious?'

'What?' says Rochelle, leaning in to get the goss.

Karmella ignores Rochelle again and laughs at me. 'You *lurve* him.'

'I do not!' I say, but I know my cheeks are bright pink.

'Haha! You are so busted,' says Rochelle with a chuckle.

I scrunch my shoulders and do a cheeky grin. 'OK, I do. But who wouldn't?'

'He's not my type,' says Karmella. 'But I can see why *you* like him.'

'Don't look now,' says Rochelle. 'He's coming over!'

I duck my head again and can't bear to look up.

'Hey, Ben,' Karmella says, loudly so everyone

can hear us. When Karmella talks everyone listens. It's like everyone in the school wants to know what we're doing, what we're up to and who we're hanging out with. I have to say that I just love it.

'Hey, yourself,' he says. 'Afternoon, ladies.' He pulls out the chair next to mine and sits. I can't believe I'm sitting next to Ben Sands. No, he's sitting next to me! 'Hi,' he says.

'Hi,' I say back. I wonder if he remembers that these were the first words we ever said to each other.

'Ahhhhh,' says Karmella, 'aren't you two sweet?'

Ben looks confused and smiles at me. 'What is she talking about?' he asks me.

I shrug. 'No idea.'

'Ben, you remember Maya, don't you?' says Karmella as if she's introducing us for the first time.

Rochelle is playing with something in her hands. She giggles up at us, so I giggle along too.

Ben rolls his eyes. 'Of course I do,' he says. 'The bombshell who arrived with a bang.'

'I arrived and fell on my backside, if that's what you mean,' I say.

Ben looks me in the eye as he laughs, and I can't

really handle the pressure of the eye contact so I look at my feet.

Rochelle starts humming the wedding march and then she throws torn up pieces of paper over us that flutter down like confetti.

'Roche!' I say, chucking a lettuce leaf at her.

'What?' Ben asks me. 'I'm not a good enough catch for you?' He's smiling, and even though I'm blushing like mad, it feels pretty good. 'Am I permitted to ask your father for your hand?'

My face falls. 'If you can find him, you can ask him.'

Everyone goes quiet for a second and I wonder if I've killed the fun.

'Well, then,' he says, 'we'll have to elope!' Suddenly he gets up, pulls me out of my chair and grabs me into a piggyback. I shriek and the whole school is looking at me and Ben and it feels fabulous. 'Come on, m'lady!'

He starts to gallop round the table with me on his back. 'Argh! Ben! Stop!' I squeal. But I don't want him to stop.

In the corner of the lunch room I catch Luke looking over. He scowls. 'Oi! Put her down! Now!' He sounds angry. Since when did Luke become the lunch monitor?

Ben looks a little scared. He lowers me to the floor and says, 'Sorry.'

'No problem,' I reply. 'Thanks for the ride.'

'Any time,' he says with a wink.

God, I don't know if Ben Sands has ever seen me when I'm not bright red with embarrassment. I just know that people will be talking about me and Ben, and hopefully – with Karmella and Rochelle's help – Ben and I will be BF-GF by the end of the day.

'So,' Ben says, sitting back down at the table and panting a little, 'what are you guys up to?'

'Nothing,' Karmella groans. 'It's so unbelievably lame round here.'

'Yeah,' I say, just to agree with her. But my life has never been more interesting than it is right now.

Rochelle scans the room as if looking for inspiration. 'If it gets any worse, we might even resort to going to that stupid poetry competition.' She points at the poster with *Searching for Shakespeare* written large. The poster I designed.

'I organized that competition!' I say. 'It's not stupid.'

'It *is* stupid, Maya,' says Rochelle.

I feel indignant for a second. But when I look round the table Karmella and Ben are nodding.

'I mean, it's sweet that you're getting involved and everything,' says Karmella, 'but everyone is laughing at you.'

I had no idea. I guess it's what Luke said about not showing people you care about things. 'Oh . . . OK . . .' I say. I hope Ben doesn't think I'm stupid. I wish Karmella hadn't said it in front of him.

'Hey, know what would be funny?' says Karmella, getting excited. 'Why don't you fix it so that weird goth girl wins?'

'Why would she do that?' asks Rochelle.

Karmella has a wicked smile on her face and I don't like it. 'Turns out her parents don't know she's a goth freak.'

'No way!' says Ben.

'Fix the competition so she wins, then we'll invite her parents along to the prize-giving ceremony. Zeba will have to choose — be a goth or be grounded for life.'

Karmella starts laughing again and Rochelle and Ben join in.

'I'm not sure,' I say.

'Why not?' she asks.

'I don't want to get her in trouble.'

'Why?' asks Karmella, looking genuinely puzzled. 'Who cares?'

'I just don't think—'

Ben comes to my rescue. 'Maya's not into mean tricks, are you, Maya?' He looks at me and I could dissolve. 'She's a good girl.'

'I'm not *that* good,' I say, raising my eyebrow, trying to be sexy.

'Glad to hear it.' He gets up from the table. 'Look, I got to go,' he says. 'Goodbye, fiancée,' he adds, picking up my hand and kissing it. I watch him as he leaves, unable to believe that just happened.

'You're in there, Maya,' says Rochelle with a congratulatory nod. 'Looks like Ben has got a *thang* for you.'

Karmella flips and glares at Rochelle. 'What would you know? Who's got a *thang* for you? Someone stupid like Billy the div, maybe.'

Oh God, please don't let Karmella bring up Billy.

Rochelle splutters, looks at me because she knows I've seen her and Billy together, then glares back at Karmella. 'What's your problem, Karmella? You've been weird with me all week.'

'Oh, nothing,' says Karmella, her head waggling like it was on a spring. 'I would tell you if I had a problem . . . Just like I know you'd tell me . . .'

I can see where this is going. I've seen it all

before with Frankie and Zeba and I don't know if I can go through it again.

'Oh, just—' says Rochelle, but I cut her off by clearing my throat.

'Um . . . Rochelle,' I say, hating the way my voice sounds all high and nervous. 'We found out about you and, um, Craig Baker.'

Rochelle's mouth falls wide open. 'I . . . What did you hear? Who told you?'

'I know you snogged him, all right!' says Karmella, and she sniffs back a tear. 'I can't believe you would do that to me.'

Time for me to step in again. 'I'm sure she didn't mean to. I'm sure it just happened.' How would I know? I wasn't there and I've never been in that situation, but it sounds like a good excuse.

'That's right, Karm,' says Rochelle, leaning forward and taking her hand. 'I didn't mean to. I promise.'

'Really?' says Karmella. She's stopped sniffing and looks up at Rochelle. That was quick – maybe she didn't like him that much after all.

'Yes, really,' says Rochelle. 'I'm sorry.'

'Oh God, don't worry.' Karmella swipes her hand in front of her face like she's not bothered. 'I used to like him a bit, but not any more. Thanks for saying sorry though.'

Rochelle hesitates before she gives Karmella a hug. Karmella hugs her right back. Wow, I fixed this before it started. Sometimes honesty is the best policy.

'Come on.' Rochelle waves me into the hug. 'You too.'

I join the hug and I can't believe how great things have got. Not only am I in with the cool group, but I've made them better friends with each other too.

'Look, guys,' says Rochelle, 'I have to go and get my stuff for PE.' She stands up and is about to walk away when she says sorry to Karmella again. 'I was an idiot.'

Karmella says nothing as Rochelle leaves.

'It looks like she meant it,' I tell Karmella.

'I don't know,' she says, looking angry again. 'I don't care anyway.'

But I know she does care. I know she isn't as tough as she makes out. Deciding that honesty is the best policy again, I take a deep breath and say, 'I know you entered a poetry competition.'

'What?' she says, and looks around to see if anyone's heard me.

'And you won.'

Karmella looks shocked and starts blinking rapidly.

'"L is heLL". You put it in the locker.'

I watch as she works out that I know everything. She looks terrified, and actually it's quite sweet.

'I think the poem is great! You shouldn't be ashamed—'

She points her finger at me. 'If you tell anyone—'

'I would never tell anyone,' I say. 'I'm your friend now, remember? Friends keep each other's secrets.'

She looks confused. 'Wow, Maya, you're actually . . . *nice*, aren't you?'

I shrug because I kind of assume that's how everyone is.

'Rochelle has been my friend for ages,' she continues, 'but even she calls me a bitch behind my back and snogs the boys I like. Not like you. You're a *real* friend.'

'Yes, Karm,' I say. I'm not sure if she's being genuine or just telling me what I want to hear. 'I want to be your real friend.'

She tilts her head to one side. 'Well, let's do that, shall we?'

She hugs me tight. Being in the cool group is going to be the best.

Then, out of the corner of my eye, I can see that Luke is still staring at me.

Chapter 27

'Maya, where do you think you're going?'

Busted.

I'm trying to sneak out after chemistry without Mr Holt noticing, but it's too late.

'Come back here, please.' Not a request. An order.

As the rest of the class leaves, they stare. One person even shouts, 'Good luck.' I've been hanging out with Karmella and Rochelle all week and now that I'm popular everyone speaks to me. I turn round slowly and look up at Mr Holt.

'Sir?' I say, in the cold, bored voice that Karmella uses.

'Where are you going?' he asks. 'We're supposed to be having a meeting about the poetry competition. Did you forget?'

'But it's Friday!' I protest.

'What about all the other meetings you've

missed?' He's using that tone that says, 'I'm not angry, I'm just confused'. The one adults always use when they are trying to *relate* to you. But no one can relate to the three weeks I've had since I started here.

I shrug. 'I forgot.'

He sighs. 'But you arranged them!'

Turns out he is angry after all. I shrug again.

He holds my gaze and then looks over at Zeba. I didn't notice she was still in the room.

'You two aren't sitting next to each other in class any more. What happened?'

I say nothing. And for the first time ever, Zeba doesn't speak either. She just looks up at me from under her heavily made-up lashes. She looks sad, and I take that as a sign that she might want to forgive me and be friends again. I dare to smile at her.

Slowly her painted red lips curl and she gives me a half-smile back.

'I'm sorry, Zeba,' I say. Then turn to Mr Holt. 'Sorry, Mr Holt.' Then I look back at Zeba. 'It won't happen again.'

Mr Holt looks relieved that he won't have to get involved and he shakes his head and carries on. 'Good, take a seat.' He motions to the seat next to Zeba.

I grin at Zeba as I sit down and she smiles — not a proper smile, but wider than before, and I know we'll be fine. Karmella and Rochelle will just have to accept that Zeba's part of our group. Now that they've learned how to be nice, I'm sure it'll all work out.

'We've made some headway with plans . . .' says Mr Holt, but he stops when the door opens.

It's Miss Draper. 'Hi, everyone,' she says. 'Am I late?'

'No, no, you're perfect. As usual,' he says.

She blushes and fumbles with her things as she puts them on the desk next to him. 'So, where were we?'

'The prize-giving is next Saturday and we need to have the logistics finalized,' starts Mr Holt.

'Yes, the logistics, yes,' Miss Draper replies like a mumbling idiot.

I get out my notepad from my bag and write something at the top of the page. Then slide it a little bit towards Zeba so she can read it.

How are you?

She reads the note and scribbles something on her own note pad.

Ok. U?

I'm OK.

Good.

She writes, then stops to think for a moment. Then she writes loads. I lean over and read it:

What happened to you? You lied to me and frankie and now we're not friends any more. I miss you. I even miss frankie, and I can't believe you would sell us both out like that. Now you're friends with karmella and Rochelle when you said they were bitches.

I take a deep breath. I don't really know what to say, but I'm happy that Zeba got it all out in the open. I write:

I was an idiot. I wanted to be cool so much I forgot about everything else.

211

Zeba looks at the piece of paper and then away into the distance. She's weighing things up, deciding if I'm good enough to be her friend, and who can blame her?

'Oh, Mr Holt,' says Miss Draper, laughing and gently touching him on the arm. 'Stop being silly!'

He laughs at her. '*I'm* being silly!? You're the one who thinks Shakespeare is better than Marlowe!' He pushes back his chair and takes her hand.

> '*Come live with me, and be my love;*
> *And we will all the pleasures prove . . .*'

'Mr Holt!' says Miss Draper. 'Here's me thinking you were all chemical formulas and Bunsen burners.'

'There's more to me than what I hide in the fume cupboard,' he says.

As he goes on I write:

What's up with those two?

I look at Zeba and she sticks her finger in her mouth, making a sick face. I hide a snigger behind my hand. Finally I can relax. Zeba has forgiven me and, if we both work at it, we can get Frankie to forgive us too.

Zeba becomes serious. She starts writing again.

I've been busy. I've been trying
to find Hillary Randle.

I shoot her an astonished look and write:

And???!!!

She looks smug and writes:

Progress . . .

I had no idea Zeba's detective skills were so good!

I've also been looking into
people called Raphael. It's not
anyone in our school.

Even though I am no longer an uncool freak, I haven't stopped thinking about that secret. I still think it's Luke's, but if no one in the school is called Raphael, how do we find out?

She's still writing:

> I looked back at the records
> for the last ten years. There
> has been never been anyone
> with that name in this school.

I have to think about this for a minute before it hits me – it makes perfect sense!

I write:

> It's definitely Luke!

She gives me a don't-be-ridiculous look. I insist:

> It is!

Zeba scrawls a giant question mark on the page.

I continue:

> Raphael must have gone to his old school.
> Maybe he broke that boy's leg to stop him
> from hurting this Raphael person!

Zeba rolls her eyes. She writes:

> Wow, Maya. I know you were the
> creative type, but this is some story.

I reply:

I reckon Luke's a hero, not a bully!

Zeba smiles at me and shakes her head in dismay.

You are <u>tragically</u> *deluded!*

Maybe she's right. I mean, I did see him picking on that boy – Angus McAllister. He was pinning him back and threatening him. What more evidence do I need? Maybe I *am* tragically deluded. I lean back on my chair as I think about it.

'Have you two got any favourite poems in the ones we've seen so far?' asks Miss Draper, who's suddenly remembered that we're here.

But something on Zeba's page catches my eye. Something about the word *tragically*. I've seen it before.

'There are a few I like,' says Zeba, but I'm hardly listening, transfixed by the word on her notebook. Written in purple ink. With a star over the *i*.

'What was the name of that one that I told you I liked, Maya?' Zeba asks me.

The new girl is tragically uncool.

I stand up and point at Zeba. 'You passed that note!'

Zeba leans back in shock. 'What?'

Mr Holt frowns at me. 'Maya, what are you talking about?'

I ignore him and continue to glare at Zeba. 'You passed the note about me on my first day!'

'Oh,' says Mr Holt. He remembers as well as I do.

'I don't know what—' Zeba says, but she's gone white. Whiter than normal.

'I know it was you!' I say, growling at her. 'I found the secret where you confessed all.'

Zeba's mouth flaps open and shut. 'I . . . I . . .'

'You must have known I'd find it eventually.'

'I thought you would tell me,' she says. 'I thought I could explain.'

'Come on, girls,' says Mr Holt. But neither of us is listening.

'So it *was* you,' I say, nodding my head. 'I can't believe you did that!' I shout.

Zeba looks at the teachers, then she pushes her chair back and runs out of the room.

I watch her go. Zeba is a complete traitor. I hate her.

'Maya,' asks Miss Draper, 'what's going on?'

Luke was right: you can't trust anyone. No wonder he's nasty to everyone. No wonder Karmella acts like she does. You have to be like that to survive. Dog eat dog.

An idea comes into my head.

'It's silly!' I say, smiling at Miss Draper. 'It's nothing.'

'Are you sure, Maya?' says Mr Holt. 'You and Zeba have been frosty with each other all week.'

'Everything is fine. In fact . . .' Time to put Karmella's plan into action. 'I'm glad I can speak to you alone because I've chosen my winner for the competition.'

'Really?' says Miss Draper. 'Who?'

'She's too modest, but I think Zeba's entry is superb.' I push Zeba's poem towards them.

Miss Draper picks up Zeba's poem and skim-reads it. 'It's outstanding,' she says with an appreciative nod. 'What do you think, Mr Holt?'

He reads it too. 'You're the expert,' he says. 'But I do think it's very good.'

'So it isn't a fix if you think she should win too,' I say. Miss Draper and Mr Holt nod in agreement. My smile broadens. 'But, so she doesn't think we've set it up, or feel awkward, let's not tell her.'

'That's nice of you, Maya,' says Miss Draper.

'And also,' I add, ready to complete my plan, 'I think it would be a good idea to invite her parents to the prize-giving. As a surprise.'

'I'm sure they'll be very proud,' says Mr Holt.

'How nice you are, Maya,' says Miss Draper.

I grin. 'What are friends for?' I say.

Chapter 28

I walk down the halls of Mount Selwyn High School, still in shock. It's after five o'clock on a Friday so luckily everyone has left for the day and no one can see how angry I am.

I hear footsteps running behind me.

'Maya! Wait!'

I wish I had some sort of magic machine that would take me away from here so I don't have to confront her. Her hand lands on my shoulder and she spins me around.

'Maya,' Zeba says, panting. 'I'm sorry.'

I scowl at her, tears filling my eyes.

'It was . . . I didn't mean it . . .' she says.

'You didn't mean it? Don't act dumber than you really are. Which is pretty dumb!' I'm learning this stuff from Karmella and Rochelle. Zeba looks like I've punched her in the stomach.

I revel in my chance to watch her squirm.

'There was only one secret that I kept from you and Frankie. I was embarrassed because it was about me.'

Zeba gulps.

'I found it at the top of the pile, just milliseconds before I first met you.'

Zeba looks at her feet.

'I remember it off by heart because I haven't stopped thinking about it.' I narrow my eyes as I look at her. 'Perhaps we could recite it together:

I passed the note about the new girl.'

Zeba sobs but I continue:

'I want Karmella to be MY friend, not her friend. The new girl is tragically uncool.'

I put extra emphasis on those last two words, so she knows how much they hurt.

'Maya——' she starts.

'You ruined everything for me here! After St Cecilia's I needed a fresh start. But you made sure that couldn't happen.'

The tears falling down her face means her make-up comes away in hideous streaks.

'You did it because you wanted to be friends with Karmella. I thought you didn't care what people thought about you. I thought you liked being weird!'

'Of course I care what people think about me!' Her eyes are squeezed shut as if she wishes she could be anywhere else but here. 'I want to be popular. I hate not having any friends just because I like strange music and dress differently.'

'So you decided to target me?'

'I'm so sorry, Maya. It was . . . I was . . . I didn't . . .'

'What?' I say, shouting now. I have never heard my voice like this. 'How can I believe one word that comes out of your lying mouth?'

'I only—'

'What the hell are you doing?' comes a voice from behind me. It's low and growling and I recognize it. I turn round and see Luke Marino walking down the corridor towards me, his fists clenched.

'Luke,' I say, 'what are you doing here?'

'Detention,' he says. 'What are you doing?!'

Zeba lets out a whimper and I turn round to see that she is backed into the wall. I am standing very close to her, my finger pointing in her face and she's crying. This doesn't look good.

I quickly take a big step back.

'Luke,' I say, 'I—'

Now that she's free, Zeba uses the opportunity

to run away down the corridor. I watch her go and wish I could follow her, but Luke has already reached me and now he's the one looking angry and threatening.

'Maya,' he says, 'when did you become such a bully?'

The b-word makes my breath catch in my throat. I try to speak. 'I'm . . . I'm not a—'

'It looks that way to me.'

Visions of those girls from St Cecilia's taunting and teasing me – their noses just inches from mine – fly through my mind. But instead of feeling scared, I feel angry.

'Why don't you mind your own business?' My anger makes me brave. 'Everyone knows who the school bully is!'

I can't believe what I've just said. I wince, squeezing my eyes shut. But when I open my eyes I see he's looking thoughtful.

'OK,' he says in a soft voice. 'You're right. I shouldn't judge you when I don't know the whole story.'

'I'm not a bully . . .' I tell him. 'I can't stand bullying.'

I remember the way those St Cecilia girls locked me in the supply cupboard and took my phone so

I couldn't get help. I remember the huge chunk Gloria Fairchild cut out of my hair in physics, so Mum had to pay for a short-short boy-cut.

'Me too,' says Luke.

Wait. What?

'If you can't stand bullying,' I say, 'why does everyone think you are one? That doesn't come from nowhere.'

Luke shakes his head. He's not going to answer the question, and the secret — *I didn't do what they think I did . . .* — comes back to me.

'I thought you and Zeba were friends,' he says.

I give a heavy sigh and let the adrenalin leak out of me. This is bad. I think I'm going to cry. 'I thought so too. But . . . you probably don't remember . . . but on my first day at Mount Selwyn, someone passed a note about me.'

'I remember,' he says, sounding sympathetic.

'It was Zeba who wrote that note. And I thought she was my friend!' I barely get out the word *friend* before the tears erupt. I cover my face with my hands, ostriching, pretending that if I can't see him, then he can't see me. Luke probably can't wait to get away from this ugly mess bawling in the hallway.

But instead I feel his arm around me. Then

his other arm. At first I'm really shocked. With my face buried deep in his chest I open my eyes to check that this is really happening and he's not trying to smother me to death. But this hug is nice. He smells of washing powder and I feel safe in his big warm arms.

After about five minutes there are no more tears left in my reservoir and I pull away, very aware of the wet patch that's appeared on Luke's shirt, a little dirty from my mascara.

I point and give him a lopsided smile. 'Sorry about that.'

He laughs. 'It's OK. My mum's cleaned off worse than a little saltwater.'

We stand there looking embarrassed because of our hug.

'Umm,' he says, shrugging and kicking at nothing on the floor. 'Do you want to go and get some chips?'

I sniffle and say, 'OK.' And Luke and I head for the door.

Only when we reach the high street do I realize: this is my first date.

Chapter 29

Luke and I are standing outside the chip shop. The sun's setting and the heat from the chips is warming my hands. There aren't that many people around, and I haven't seen anyone from Mount Selwyn. That's probably a good thing.

I pick up a chip with the wooden fork, blow on it and pop it in my mouth.

Luke shoves in a forkful of chips and then starts huffing and blowing. 'Ah . . . Oh . . . Mww- where're a bwwit hwwot!'

I laugh. 'I can't understand you with your mouth full,' I say.

He huffs a little more, then finally manages to swallow. 'Well, excuuuse me,' he says.

Those are the first words we've spoken to each other in a while and we fall back into silence. It's weird how silence can be quite a good way to bond.

He turns to me and he suddenly goes all shy.

'So . . . um . . . Maya . . . Do you have a boy-friend?'

Is Luke asking me out?! What should I say? 'Oh, I *did* have a boyfriend. But—'

'Hitachi,' he says. And when he sees my surprised expression he adds, 'I saw him on your Facebook.'

'Oh, yes, well . . .' I say. So Luke's actually been looking at my Facebook page. 'Well, it doesn't matter now because we broke up. We were finding the distance too hard to deal with.' I'm trying my best to sound mature. 'I'm here, he's there. I need to move on, you know. I can't—'

'Word of advice, Maya,' Luke says, interrupting me with a cheeky grin. 'When you pick a photo of a fake boyfriend, don't use the star player of the England under-21 rugby team.'

'What?!' My blushing has turned the air warm.

'Your Hitachi's real name is Ginjiro Ito, and he's an up-and-coming star on the rugby scene.'

I am mortified! He knew I was lying all along. I cover my face with my free hand.

'You must think I'm such an idiot!' I squeal through my fingers.

He just laughs. 'I'll let you off.'

I shake my head. 'I was trying to make myself

seem cool and I've made myself look even more foolish than I was in the first place.'

'Everyone does it, Maya,' he says. And he's being so sweet that I dare to look at him through my fingers. He goes on. 'We all have secrets.'

'Even you?' I ask.

He shrugs and nods at the same time. This is the moment to ask him about whether he's a bully. Now I can find out about Raphael. I take a deep breath and say, 'Do you mind if I ask what happened at your old school?'

Luke frowns and I wonder if I have made a mistake. He shuffles and coughs for a second before saying, 'What did you hear?'

'Umm, I heard that you beat someone up and put them in hospital.'

'Oh,' he says, with a sad sort of smile that I can't work out. 'Well, that's not what happened.'

He didn't do what everyone thinks he did.

'So, um, so why do you let people think that?' I ask, hoping that he is going to tell me about Raphael.

But Luke just shrugs again. He doesn't say a word and he eats a chip so he doesn't have to look at me.

'Tell me,' I plead. 'I won't tell anyone.'

He sighs. He looks at me then back down at his chips, and for a moment I think he's not going to say anything. But then he says, 'I didn't have detention this afternoon.'

With all the stuff going on with Zeba I forgot that he said he had a detention.

'I was seeing a counsellor.'

He looks at me to see how I'm going to react. Like everyone else, he is scared of what people think. He lies to protect himself too. I wonder if the counsellor is the one who gives him the happy pills.

'Oh,' I say, thinking that this is a moment for that *less is best* proverb that Grandpa uses.

'Yeah. I went through a lot of stuff last year, and the school thought it would be good if I saw a counsellor to, you know, sort out a few things in my head.'

'What kind of things?'

'I don't know.' He looks really uncomfortable. 'Like, maybe, not everything is to do with me. I don't need to fix the world's problems by myself.'

'You were trying to fix me just now,' I say, 'when you thought I was bullying Zeba. But I saw you bullying Angus McAllister with my own eyes.'

Luke winces. 'Yeah, but you didn't see what Angus did to Amanda Curran.'

'Huh?'

'He tripped her up and knocked her books and cello to the floor.'

I *do* remember that happening, just before we posted that note in her locker, and I remember poor Amanda looked mortified.

'So I shoved him up against the lockers and told him to apologize.'

I take a deep breath and try to make sense of everything. Looks like I was right: Luke's a kind of hero.

'You're trying to help people,' I say. 'But I thought your counsellor said it's not your job to fix things.'

He looks into the distance. 'Yeah. And sometimes there are things you can't help, no matter what you do.'

I seize the moment. 'Is this something to do with Raphael?'

Luke's head whips round so fast that I almost fall backwards. 'What did you say?'

'Raphael,' I say. 'Do you put on this hard-man act to protect him?'

He takes a step towards me. 'Don't you

dare . . .' His eyes narrow. 'How do you know about Raphael?'

That's the one thing I can't tell him. 'I . . .'

'Don't you ever mention his name,' he says, his eyes blazing. He throws his chips on the floor.

But I can't give up now. If I can get Luke to open up then I can help him. 'I want to fix people too! Tell me about Raphael and we—'

'I told you not to say his name!' he growls at me.

But for some reason I'm not scared. 'Why won't you tell me?'

Luke opens his mouth to say something . . . and then he stops . . . and closes he mouth again. And instead of saying another word, he turns and walks away down the high street.

Chapter 30

I've never bunked off anything. And I never thought I would *ever* bunk off English. But after what happened on Friday night I don't want to face Luke. Me and Karmella and Roche are in the toilets hiding from the teachers.

'I love that shade of lipgloss on you, Maya,' says Rochelle.

I shrug. 'I felt it was a bright-red kinda day, you know?' I say.

Karmella laughs. 'You go, girl!'

I hand Rochelle the lipgloss. 'You can keep it if you like, I have loads!'

'Are you sure?'

'Yeah, sure,' I say, and wave it away as if it's nothing.

Karmella nods along. 'Maya has loads of make-up and cool clothes.' Karmella and me spent all weekend trying on clothes and looking at the secrets and talking about getting me together with Ben. Rochelle doesn't know about locker 62. We decided it should just be between me and Karm.

'I'd love to come round some time,' says Rochelle. 'If that's OK?'

'Of course.' So this is what cool feels like. Rochelle Jenkins is begging to come over. How brilliant is that? 'My mum taught me this thing,' I say. 'It's a bit lame but it makes you feel great.'

Both Rochelle and Karmella look at me with interest.

'It's called the lipgloss pep talk: you apply the lipgloss,' I add another coat, looking in the mirror, 'and repeat the words you want to feel.' I can't use *'Cool is everything'* in front of them. And Frankie's mantra — *'Just be yourself and they will all love you'* — is useless. I've replaced it with something more effective: 'Don't let anyone stand in your way.'

Karmella and Rochelle nod.

'I love it!' says Karmella. 'Your mum is awesome.'

Karmella smiles at me, and in the mirror I see Rochelle has seen us smiling and looks hurt. I decide to include her. 'We were talking about Mark Nowicki and Amanda Curran,' I say.

'Why were you talking about those freaks?' she asks. It's amazing how much time Karmella and Rochelle spend insulting people.

'They reckon they are the hottest new couple,' Karmella says. 'Yuck! You can't turn a corner without seeing them snogging each other's faces off.'

'Hideous,' says Rochelle.

'That's what I think,' says Karmella.

'It's disgusting!' I say. Although secretly I'm quite proud – both of getting Amanda and Mark together and the fact that Karmella and Rochelle are using my word.

The bell goes for break and the three of us walk out of the toilets. We link arms as we get into the corridor. People have to jump out of the way when we stride through, and they stare at us as we pass.

Ahead of us I see Cassandra Myles talking to a group of her friends. Karmella calls out to her. 'Hey, Cassandra!'

Cassandra turns round, sees Karmella and smiles at her. Everyone else looks too, wondering why Karmella is talking to Cassandra Myles.

'Hi, Kar—'

Karmella reaches forward and lifts the hem of Cassandra's skirt!

Cassandra looks shocked and panicked and tries to hold down her skirt at the front, but Karmella manages to pull it up at the back so her bum's showing.

'Put some knickers on!' Karmella shouts.

Everyone screams with laughter. One boy starts slapping his thighs as he laughs hysterically. I start laughing too, but when I see Cassandra's face I stop. She's gone bright red and she looks like she's about to cry. She runs off to the toilet.

'Oh my God,' says Roche. 'How did you know she wasn't wearing knickers?'

Karmella taps her nose. 'A little bird,' she says. Then she gives my arm a big squeeze.

Beside the door to the playground I see Zeba. She stares at me and Karmella and Rochelle: my new best friends. I turn away from her, stick my head in the air and walk on past.

We walk out to an even bigger audience. There's a load of boys playing football, but every single one of them stops what they're doing to look at us.

'Why don't you take a picture?' I say. 'It lasts longer.'

They pretend to go back to playing football,

but really I know they are looking at me – I mean *us*. I try to walk sexily, wiggling my hips a little as I stroll. And even though Frankie hasn't spoken to me in over a week, I can hear her words in my head – *mysterious and alluring*. I've finally done it.

The moment's gone and now we're standing in the cold with nothing to do. 'Oh, look, there's Ben,' says Karmella, pointing over to where he's hanging by the goal.

'He looks so dreamy when he's watching the ball,' I say.

'Careful,' Karmella says to me. 'That's my boyfriend you're talking about.'

'What?!' Did I hear her right?

'Oh, I forgot to tell you – me and Ben are going out.'

There's a sudden pain in my chest. 'Ben Sands? Are you joking?'

'No, we got together over the weekend.'

But she can't have. We spent half of this week-end talking about *me* getting with him.

'That boy is such a good kisser!'

They've *kissed*!?

'And you should have seen his face when I said I'd be his girlfriend.'

I swallow back the huge lump in my throat. 'But . . . you said . . . You knew I liked him. You said you'd get me and him—'

'Come on, Maya,' she says. 'I'm not a miracle worker!'

Rochelle laughs.

'Besides, all's fair in love and war, right?'

She walks over to Ben and he stops playing and runs over. They snog and I have to look away because it hurts too much.

'Hi, gorgeous,' he says to her.

'Hi, babe,' she says, and kisses him again.

I'm confused. Karmella's always said that Ben was too immature. She knew I liked him. And she was upset with Rochelle for doing exactly the same thing with Craig Baker that she's doing to me right now.

'What're you ladies up to?' Ben asks.

I'm too shocked to speak.

'Shall we see if anyone's down the dark path?' says Rochelle.

There are two huts in the playground, with an alleyway in between them which everyone calls the dark path. It's a favourite spot for smokers and snoggers. They start walking over and I follow them like an old woman's shopping cart, sniffing back my tears, angling my face away from them so they can't see me cry.

We get to the dark path and Amanda and Mark are halfway down there kissing like mad.

'Oh yuck!' shouts Karmella. 'I did not need to see that!'

Mark and Amanda stop kissing and look back at us. And because of Karmella's outburst a lot of other people are watching us too. Amanda wipes her face with her hand, but she's grinning from ear to ear.

'God, Mark,' says Karmella, 'you weren't wrong when you said that Amanda's kisses are sloppy!'

Mark's jaw drops and Amanda looks crushed. 'What did you say?' she asks.

'Oh, he was telling me all about your sloppy kisses last week,' says Karmella. 'When Rochelle was showing him how kissing *should* be done.' Karmella winks at Rochelle.

Amanda steps out of the dark path into the light of the playground. When everyone sees her they all go, 'Ooooo!'

'Karm——' I say. I have to get her to stop.

Amanda frowns at Karmella, then at Rochelle,

then turns to Mark. 'Did you meet up with Rochelle last week?' she asks Mark.

'No!' he says.

'Errr. Yes,' says Karmella.

Amanda's face does the green-pink-green thing, but this time it doesn't look cute. 'Did you, Mark?' she asks again, and from behind her glasses I see her eyes flash with anger. Then her bottom lip starts to tremble.

I dash forward. 'No, she didn't really!' I say. 'Karm was joking,' I tell her, hoping to end the joke before it gets out of hand. I turn round to face the school. 'Only joking, guys. Nothing happened with Rochelle and Mark.'

'Yeah, right!' comes a heckle from behind us.

'I promise, Amanda,' I tell her.

Amanda looks at Mark.

'I wouldn't call a 45-minute snog a joke,' says Karmella.

I hold my head in my hands as people start laughing and wolf-whistling.

Amanda scowls at Karmella. 'I don't believe you.' Her lip is trembling much worse now and she's starting to cry. 'Mark?'

He looks bewildered. 'She's lying,' he says. 'I swear!'

Ben guffaws.

A girl shouts at Amanda, telling her not to be an idiot.

'Amanda,' I start, 'listen—'

'Rochelle did you a favour, Amanda,' says Karmella. 'She even persuaded him to pluck his nipple hairs rather than shaving them.' Now Mark's jaw drops even lower. 'You should be thanking her.'

The crowd gasps. With this final piece of evidence Amanda runs off. Mark is too shocked to move, not understanding how any of this could have happened. I feel awful. I let Karmella into a secret that I wasn't even supposed to know myself, and she used it to be mean.

Grabbing Karmella's arm, I lead her away, and Ben and Rochelle follow. I feel all the eyes on me – on *us* – but this time I don't like it. One girl even mouths the word *bitch* to us as we pass. She's exactly right.

Billy Beckworth runs over. 'Hey, Roche,' he says, 'what just happened?'

Karmella looks at Rochelle and shakes her head in disgust, but if Rochelle notices she doesn't let her smile fall.

'Hi, Billy,' she says in a dreamy way.

Karmella coughs to remind Rochelle who she's talking to.

'Did you really kiss Mark?' Billy asks, looking hurt. 'I thought—'

'Look, Billy,' says Karmella, 'we have places to be, people to see. If you wouldn't mind stepping a good few metres out of the way — and maybe taking a shower once in a while — we'd all really appreciate it.'

My head starts to spin. I think I am going to vomit. How can I make this right?

Billy's face falls. He frowns at Karmella. 'No need to be nasty, Karmella,' he says. And I see that Billy has backbone. More backbone than me. 'Maybe your friends don't feel the same way about me as you do.' He looks at Rochelle.

Rochelle tries to hold his gaze but can't do it for more than a second. She chickens out and looks at the floor. It turns out Rochelle doesn't have backbone either.

'Face it, Billy,' says Karmella, 'you're a div. That's why everyone calls you Billy the div.'

Ben laughs.

Billy stares at Karmella. 'I'd rather be a div than a cow,' he says.

Karmella straightens up.

'Hey!' Ben growls. 'Watch what you say about my girlfriend.'

Karmella smiles sweetly so I know it's going to be bad. 'It's OK, Ben.' She turns her head slowly to Rochelle and, still smiling, she asks her, 'What do you think, Rochelle? Do you think I'm a cow, or do you think Billy is a div?'

Rochelle says nothing for a moment. Billy looks at her. I look at her, willing her to do the right thing and tell Billy she didn't kiss Mark. Surely, as a friend, Rochelle could ask Karmella not to be so horrible. But now I realize that Karmella's getting Rochelle back for kissing Craig Baker. Now I realize that this thing between me, Karmella and Rochelle is not friendship. It's something else. And it's hideous.

Rochelle raises her head. 'I wouldn't be seen dead with a div like you, Billy,' she says. 'Now get out of my way.'

Billy says nothing but I can see his heart crumble inside his chest. Just like we made Amanda's and Mark's hearts crumble. I have the power of the secrets and I gave it up to become a bully.

As Billy walks away I whisper, 'I need to go to the toilet. I feel sick.'

Rochelle says, 'Me too.'

We head to the place where every girl goes when she needs to cry. I can hear Rochelle weeping in the cubicle next to mine.

On the way out I am too disgusted to look in the mirror.

Chapter 31

I'm upstairs in my room. I'm avoiding all calls from Karmella and Rochelle, trying not to think about what we did yesterday. The only person I have left to talk to is my diary. It's the only place I can say how rubbish I'm feeling.

But where is it? I'm sure it was under my bed somewhere.

'Maya!'

It's Gran! I haven't seen her in ages and I run downstairs and throw myself into her arms.

'Oof!' she says as I almost knock her off her feet. 'What's this all about?'

'I've missed you,' I tell her, which is only half of it. Mum hasn't been her usual chirpy self since the visit to the hospital last week. She's been all spacey and weird and it's been freaking me out.

'We thought we'd stop by on our way to the supermarket. Do you want to come with?'

I nod. We haven't had any proper food in the house for days. 'Is Mum coming?' I ask.

Gran shakes her head. 'But your grandfather is.' She turns to Grandpa, who's sniffing the dead flowers in the plant pot. Gran wags her finger at him. 'But no surfing the supermarket trolleys.'

'I wasn't even senile when I did that,' he says, crossing his arms and seeming sulky.

'I know!' says Gran.

I make a shopping list, call goodbye to Mum, and we head out to the shops.

While Grandpa and I make slow laps up and down the aisles, Gran dashes off and gets the things from the list. We're in the clothes section and Grandpa picks up a pair of bright red corduroys.

'What do you think of these, Maya?' he says.

'I think they would make very nice dishcloths if you cut them up into pieces.'

He puts his hands on his hips. '*I* would wear them,' he says.

'Exactly!'

He laughs. 'I remember that your mother used to have a pair of these when she was about your age. Before . . . you know . . .'

He tails off. I know he means before she had me.

We don't really talk about that time. I guess it must have been really hard having a daughter who was thirteen and pregnant. But the most unbelievable thing is that Mum would ever wear trousers like that!

'What was Mum like when she was my age?' I ask.

'Just like you,' says Grandpa. 'She didn't have a lot of friends. And she always had her head in a book.'

I laugh it off. 'Thanks, Grandpa! Just like me: unpopular and bookish!' I'm glad to hear that me and Mum were alike at some time, though I can't believe she was ever uncool.

But something Grandpa said doesn't make any sense; if Mum was so unpopular, wearing red cords that could never have been trendy, then how did she get a boyfriend? How did she and my dad get together?

'Grandpa,' I say, my heart racing as I brace myself for asking the most serious question I have ever asked, the one that I have never asked because I've been too scared to hear the answer, 'what was my dad like?' And then the most important question of all: 'Do you remember his name?'

Grandpa picks up a pair of slippers with rabbits

on the front and frowns at them. 'We never met him,' he says. 'We never knew your mum was pregnant.'

'What?'

'These look tasty,' he says, talking about the slippers.

Grandpa's losing it again. He's blocked out mum's pregnancy and now he's trying to eat slippers. Why does my family have to be so mental?

'You didn't know Mum was pregnant?'

'Not until she brought you back from the hospital,' he says. 'Maybe we should have rabbit stew for dinner.'

I sigh. 'I'll go get apples,' I tell him and stomp away from the clothes section, past the stationery and the books, and head over to fruit and veg. I never get a straight answer from any of my family. Mum and Gran won't tell me the truth, and Grandpa only spouts complete madness about not knowing my mum was pregnant.

But there was something about the way he said it: like he wasn't lying.

Ducking behind the mound of potatoes, I decide to hide out here.

'Are you OK, love?' asks a woman pushing a

trolley packed high with power bars. She seems sweet but she looks really tired too, dark circles under her eyes.

I am momentarily mesmerized because I have never seen so many power bars in one place. 'I'm . . . I'm fine, thanks,' I say.

'Well, as long as you're sure,' she says.

I turn and walk slowly down the next aisle, where I see a very familiar silhouette. He's looking at the trays and trays of pears, counting them out with his fingers like he belongs in remedial class.

It's Luke.

And he's holding hands with someone.

He's holding hands with an older man.

Is Luke gay?

Luke looks up and sees me and instantly drops the hand of the man he was holding on to. Then the man follows Luke's gaze, turns towards me and says, 'What are you looking at, Lukie?'

Suddenly the penny drops.

'Are you looking at that pretty girl?' asks the man. 'She *is* very pretty.'

The man is clearly disabled. Down's syndrome or something. He smiles at me and his smile is just like Luke's.

This man is Luke's brother.

'Maya,' says Luke, looking shocked to see me.

I just stare at him. I don't mean to be rude, but this is so unexpected.

'Maya,' he says again, 'I'm so sorry about Friday.'

The woman with the tired eyes comes over and I get a strong smell of washing powder. She looks from me to Luke. 'Hello,' she says, and her voice is so gentle. 'Are you one of Luke's friends?'

'I . . . Hello . . . I'm . . .' I have forgotten my own name again.

'Are you Maya?' she asks.

How come *she* knows my name?

'I . . . er . . . have to go,' I say. I give her a half-smile and turn to walk away.

But just as I'm backing down the aisle I hear her saying to Luke, 'Did something happen with Raphael?'

Raphael is Luke's brother.

I walk out from the supermarket and try to get some air. This is all too much to take in. My mum is about to have a baby and she's gone insane. But then, according to Grandpa, she concealed the pregnancy with me – which might explain why she's so clueless at all the appointments. Seeing Luke and

Raphael is just the final straw. I need someone to talk to, now more than ever, and I know my diary won't cut it this time.

I need a new plan to get my friends back.

Chapter 32

It's Saturday night. I'm standing in the wings of the school stage, looking out at all the people. It's more than I expected for a Saturday night, and definitely more than I expected for a poetry competition.

I've worked out a plan to fix everything. It's pretty drastic. I really hope it works.

Mr Holt's done his 'Thank you all for coming' speech while Miss Draper is standing up there next to him, smiling. Then she talks about how important poetry can be for teenagers' emotional development.

I see Mum, who has used her huge belly to get seats for her, Gran and Grandpa, right at the front.

But I can't see Zeba anywhere. She must come; she *has to* come.

A couple arrives. As soon as I see their faces I know who they are: olive-skinned, the man has a moustache and a kind face, and the woman is wearing a headscarf and her eyes are twinkling as she looks around. Even without the heavy make-up and overblown goth get-up, I can tell who they are. Zeba's eyes are identical to his, and she has her mum's cheeky grin. They look so anxious and proud.

My stomach lurches as I see Karmella walking along the back of the hall. I haven't spoken to her since the thing in the playground, and I've avoided all her calls. She's walking towards the equipment closet for some reason.

Then my stomach lurches twice as hard as I see why she's heading there: Karmella's found Zeba, who's hiding in the equipment closet. Karmella walks over and her expression is so nasty as she whispers in Zeba's ear. Zeba's face falls, and the more Karmella says the more terrified Zeba looks. Then Zeba spots her parents by the doorway, and even through the pale make-up I can tell that the real colour has drained from her face. Karmella walks back with a smug grin.

Someone taps me on the shoulder and I spin around. It's Todd Swift, the poet who has come as a guest speaker to our poetry night. He's holding a few papers in his hand, must be his speech. 'Are you Maya?' he whispers in a Canadian accent.

'Yes, Mr Swift, it's an honour . . .' I'm a little star-struck. He's a pretty famous poet. For a poet that's not dead.

'Please, call me Todd,' he says. 'And the honour is all mine! The standard of these poems is very high. I can't wait to announce the winner. Zeba Khan – is that how I pronounce her name?'

'Yes, but—' I try to interrupt him, but he's not listening.

'Her poem is excellent. It shows such potential.'

I feel proud of my friend. 'I'm sure she'll be pleased to hear that, Mr— er, Todd. But—'

Now he interrupts me, glancing down at his papers and up again. 'So, I give a short talk about poetry and then I tell everyone who's won, is that right?'

'Yes, please.' I take a deep breath and launch my plan into action. 'But if it's OK with you, I would like to announce the winner myself.'

He shrugs. 'Whatever you prefer.'

Miss Draper turns to us. 'So,' she says, reaching her arm out to welcome Todd, 'without further ado, here is tonight's guest speaker: Todd Swift!'

The hall erupts into applause as Todd walks on to the stage, giving an awkward wave. 'Thanks. Thanks, everyone.' He stands at the podium and shuffles his papers. 'I'm pleased to see so many here tonight when you could have been at home watching Saturday-night TV.' There's a quiet chuckle from the audience. 'This is a great time in your life to start writing poetry. Poetry purges the soul of agony, and, let's face it, the teenage years are the most agonizing of them all!'

Another little laugh and I laugh too, proud that I made such a great choice of speaker.

'Poetry has come a long way since sonnets and iambic pentameter . . .' he's saying.

Movement from the other side of the stage, where Miss Draper and Mr Holt are standing, catches my attention. Hidden behind the curtain, Miss Draper's little finger is grabbing on to Mr Holt's little finger!

It's taking a second to sink in. Then I screech, 'O! M! G!'

Todd stops speaking for a second and turns to look at me. The whole school hall goes quiet as they wonder what on earth that noise was.

'Sorry,' I say to Todd.

Miss Draper and Mr Holt are together! It must be down to us a little bit, because of the poetry competition, and that makes me feel so happy.

Turns out that adults act like teenagers all the time, and adults have secrets too.

I take their happiness as an omen that everything is going to go perfectly tonight.

'. . . Maya Andrews!' says Todd.

It's my cue to come on and do my thing. I walk out on to the stage and my mum whoops and cheers and gets everyone all stirred up for my entrance. Grandpa shouts, 'Come on, you Spurs!' Obviously a little confused, but no one pays any attention because everyone is looking at me.

I smile at them all and wave as I walk up to the podium and step forward to the mic.

'Hello. Er . . . hi . . . everyone,' I say. I feel a little nervous, seeing all these faces looking up at me. But I remember Frankie's lipgloss pep talk — *Just be yourself and they will all love you* — and I push on. I don't even need the lipgloss.

'There were loads of great entries to the poetry competition,' I say, impressed that I'm only stammering a little. 'All of them expressed something new and surprising. Unfortunately though, there can only be one winner . . .'

Karmella is bouncing up and down, pointing over at Zeba and laughing. Zeba's peeking out from behind the closet door, holding her face in her hands.

'The winner today showed such heart and raw emotion that we couldn't *not* give it to her.'

Karmella stares at Zeba, waiting for the bomb to drop.

'That winner is . . . Karmella Loughton.'

Chapter 33

A few of the parents start clapping, but most of the students are too stunned to join in.

'Karmella Loughton has won with her fabulous poem —' I catch Karmella's eye as I say — 'L is heLL.'

Karmella stares at me as if she might kill me. Then she quickly glances at people round the room, wondering how they are going to react, wondering when they are going to laugh at her.

No one does.

Zeba sticks her head out from behind the equipment closet. She smiles at me and mouths, 'Thank you,' and I smile back. Not wanting to draw too much attention to her in case her parents see, but wanting to let her know that I will never do anything mean ever again.

I take a deep shaky breath. 'If I may, I would like to read it for you now.'

My mum's face is lit up with pride. Or maybe it's pregnancy glow.

I take Karmella's poem out and start reading.

> L.
> L is heLL.
> Neither first to be caLLed
> nor best saved tiLL Last
> always Lost in the middLe . . .

I read the poem to the end, looking right into Karmella's eyes as I say the last line.

> . . . they've never heard my words.

I hope I've done Karmella's poem justice. The hall is silent for a moment before the clapping begins. A lot of people turn to look at Karmella, all of them smiling. Karmella has gone a little red but she must be pleased at the response.

I wait for it to quieten down before I say, 'I know,' (because I've read so many of your secrets) 'that everyone has felt exactly like this at one time or another. I would like to thank Karmella personally for writing it because I think it helps all of us to know that we are not alone.

'Karmella —' I stretch out my hand to her — 'would you like to say anything to the school as you come up and get your prize?'

There is another long pause as I wait for Karmella to run with glee to the front of the hall, jump up the steps to the podium and tell everyone that it's OK to be upset once in a while. That being a bit weird and feeling lonely does not make you uncool. But Karmella is scowling. Slowly a smile creeps on to her face and she gets up from her chair and walks towards the front. The crowd starts applauding again as she sashays over, like a model on a catwalk. She carries her bag in one hand and I wonder why she's bringing it with her. She takes the steps one at a time.

Everyone has got tired of clapping so Karmella crosses the stage in complete silence, apart from the occasional cough or shuffle. She pushes past me to get to the podium, covers the microphone with her hand and whispers, 'You're going to get it now.'

Oh God.

'Thank you, Maya,' Karmella says loudly into the mic. 'That was very sweet of you.'

I nod at her and smile back, the sides of my mouth wobbling.

'I want to thank Maya on behalf of everyone, in fact.'

Mum beams up at me. Gran and Mum hold hands. They seem so happy to be here, but I wish that they weren't. I don't know what's about to happen, but I don't think it will be good.

'Maya Andrews has thrown this whole thing together, trying to get us in touch with our emotions,' she says. 'Almost as if she wants to make us expose our secrets to the whole world.'

People have no idea where this speech is going. Some start to laugh nervously.

'Don't you think, Mr Swift –' she turns to Todd, who looks a little shocked to be included in her performance – 'that the best poems expose the truth, about ourselves and how we feel about others.'

'Yes, I suppose—' replies Todd, having to shout because he doesn't have a microphone.

But Karmella cuts him off. 'Why would Maya want us to know each other's secrets? Why would sweet little Maya Andrews care so much? Because she is such a *nice* person.'

Why does she say '*nice*' like it's a bad thing? I can hardly look at my mum's face as it falls from pride to complete confusion.

Karmella turns to me. 'Maya, you asked if I had something to say to these lovely people, and I do.'

I back my way into the wings, but I can't stop watching.

'Not many of you know this, but Maya is a poet too. I'd like to read out something of hers now.'

The sinking feeling's just got worse. She reaches down into her bag and pulls out a pretty notepad with an embroidered flower design on the front. A diary. And it's one I recognize very well.

'It's more prose poetry, but you'll get into it as it goes on. This poem is called "Making up a boyfriend"!'

Big guffaws of laughter rip through the room. Miss Draper looks at me, ready to hear my secret poem. I mouth at Miss Draper, 'Please stop her.' But she gives me a thumbs up and an encouraging smile.

Karmella continues in a fake posh accent that she has adopted to mimic me. *Me and Mum made a fake boyfriend today to fool everyone into thinking I am cool.*

I hide my face in my hands.

We've spent ages on him and he's so hot that

I wish he really did exist. But if he did, what are the chances he would fall for someone ugly and stupid like me?'

Titters rise from the audience.

Karmella continues. *'I will never be cool or sexy like my mum. She's always telling me how important it is to be cool. I must be such a disappointment.'*

My mum blushes and people start to point her out. Gran frowns and Mum covers her mouth with her hand.

'I know what you are all thinking, right: this is the sweetest mother-and-daughter relationship you have ever seen.' Karmella waits for the audience to die down again before she continues. 'But wait, this poem gets better.'

Oh no. This is it.

'I know Mum is heartbroken about breaking up with Dave. But she also hates him too. Maybe now she hates him as much as I do.'

Mum's head snaps up when she hears Dave's name.

Miss Draper sees the panic on my face and I think she's just realized what's going on. She walks on to the stage so Karmella starts speaking really quickly.

'She dumped him because he accused her of

261

throwing away his engagement ring, then lying about it.'

Miss Draper gets to Karmella and puts her hand out for my diary. 'Thank you, Karmella, that's enough now.'

Karmella ignores Miss Draper and carries on reading. *'The thing is, she didn't throw away Dave's engagement ring . . .'*

Miss Draper takes the diary from Karmella and grabs her by the arm. But Karmella has enough time to lean forward and say two words into the mic:

'I did.'

Silence.

Miss Draper leads Karmella past me. She says, 'You are in a lot of trouble, young lady,' but Karmella doesn't seem to care. She grins at me with her teeth clenched.

Mum looks like she's in a nightmare she can't get out of. I know how she feels. She clutches her belly and gets up. Then she waddles out of the hall, her mouth grimacing in pain and tears running down her face.

When we were living in Denham, Mum took off her engagement ring and left it by the sink. I found it. Then something came over me. I didn't want Mum to marry Dave. Mum, Dave and the new baby would be a real family, and where would I be? I would be the odd one out. So I ran to the local park and I chucked the ring in the river.

'Mum!' I call after her, but she doesn't look back.

'Maya,' Gran shouts, 'how could you?!'

But I can't deal with Gran right now. I can't deal with Mr Holt and the audience. And I definitely can't deal with Todd Swift, who looks as if he's been placed in a busy airport on a snowy day and told to sort everyone out.

I turn and run down the stairs. I have to find Mum and explain everything.

Trouble is, I don't know where to start.

Chapter 34

Mum's not answering her mobile.

I run out of the hall, not caring what anyone is saying about me or whether anyone is following. I have to find Mum and apologize for letting her take the blame about the engagement ring and ruining her life. Again.

I start running down the corridors, wondering where my mum would have gone after hearing the news that her daughter, her sweet dream, is a lying, deceitful cow. First I run to locker 62. It doesn't make sense, but I hoped she might have come to the place where all the secrets come out. But of course she doesn't know it's mine, and she's not here.

I bang my head against the stupid thing. It's not my fault that I got given locker 62, but everything else is my fault. I feel terrible about what I've done: about Frankie and Zeba, about Dave and the ring, about everything. But then I think back to Hillary Randle, the person who started this whole thing. She made mistakes and she ran away from them. I'm not going to run away from mine. I'm going to be brave like my mum.

Suddenly I know where she is: the place where every girl goes when she needs to cry. I start with the toilets by the gym and I can hear her as soon as I push the door.

She's crying, but she's also moaning too.

'Mum!' I shout.

'Argh!' she screams.

I round the corner and see her crouched over in a shower cubicle. She's clutching her stomach and her face is screwed up in agony.

'Mum! Are you OK? Is the baby coming?'

But Mum says nothing. Nothing intelligible anyway. It sounds like, 'This is where it should happen . . .' She's spouting complete drivel: 'It makes sense now . . . I'm here . . . and Hillary Randle . . .'

Did she just say *Hillary Randle?* How does Mum know Hillary Randle? I run and sit beside her on the damp shower floor, not caring that it's soaking through my skirt. I take her hand. 'Are you OK, Mum?'

She looks in my eyes and says, 'This is where we first met.'

Mum's face is like Grandpa's on his worst days. On the days when he's forgotten who he is and he's scared of us and his surroundings. Mum yells as another contraction comes.

'Mum!' I shout, and her eyes roll back in her head.

I'm so scared. I can't look after Mum. Not when she's like this. I dial 999.

'Which service do you require?' asks the woman on the phone.

'My mum's having a baby! We're at Mount Selwyn High School!'

'All right, love. It's OK,' says the woman on the phone. 'I'm sending an ambulance to you now. Are you on your own?'

I nod and start to cry as I realize I am completely on my own.

'Is there anyone you can call?'

I think about Gran, but she doesn't have a mobile, and besides, I don't think she likes me very much right now. There *is* someone I can call. He said he would always be there for me if I needed him and I know he would make me feel safe.

I hang up on the 999 woman and find his number in my phone.

'Maya?' he says. 'Are you OK?'

I feel relieved at just the sound of his voice. 'No, I'm not. Mum's gone into labour and I'm all by myself with her,' I say, sucking in my breath through the sobs.

'Where are you?' he asks.

'At school,' I say. 'In the girls' showers.'

'OK, don't worry. I'm coming now.'

I breathe a sigh of relief. 'Thanks, Dave.'

And suddenly I don't feel alone any more.

Chapter 35

Dave and I stand round Mum's hospital bed, each holding one hand as she rests her eyes. We've been here for sixteen hours; all night. The doctors said that the baby wouldn't be coming for a while and they have given her something to help her sleep.

Dave reaches over and strokes my head. 'You did great.'

'Dave, I'm so sorry about the ring,' I tell him. 'I didn't want you to marry Mum. I didn't think you were good enough for her. But now . . .'

He smiles at me. 'What do you think now?'

'I think you're OK,' I say.

'Thanks,' he says.

'And you're just the sort of man my mum needs. Sensible. You'll look after her.'

'I will,' he says.

We both look at Mum for a bit. She looks peaceful.

'I better call your gran and grandpa,' he says.

He's been calling them every half-hour with updates. It was the only way to get them to stay away. But as Dave goes to leave, a doctor comes in.

'Good morning,' he says. 'We need to wake her up now. I think it's time to try pushing.'

The doctor gently puts a hand on Mum's shoulder and wakes her. Dave looks nervous, but also excited. Like he can't wait to meet his new son. As soon as Mum's eyes open she looks terrified.

'I think you'd better leave the room for this bit,' the doctor says to me.

I nod and swallow past the lump in my throat as I run to give Mum a kiss. 'Good luck, Mum,' I say. 'You'll do great.' Repeating what Dave said to me.

She still looks bewildered. As if she has no idea what is happening to her, or why. 'I can't do this,' she says. She looks first at me, standing next to her, then at the doctor.

Dave rushes to her side. 'It's natural to feel scared, Leanne,' he says. 'But it's going to be fine.'

'Yes,' says the doctor in a chirpy way. 'Besides, it's always easier the second time round.'

'I've never done this before,' Mum says in a daze.

The drugs must be hitting her harder than we thought.

Dave turns to the doctor and tries to whisper, 'She's been like this for a while. Confused, like she's a little delirious. Is that normal?'

The doctor's frown shows he's taking this seriously, but he doesn't look panicked. 'It can happen,' he says. 'Shock affects people in different ways. We'll keep a good eye on her.'

'I've never given birth before,' Mum blurts out. 'Tell me what to do!'

Why is Mum saying this? I suppose she's gone into shock, like the doctor said, but she doesn't look as crazy as she did before.

'It was a long time ago that you had Maya,' says Dave, 'but your body remembers, even if you don't—'

'But I didn't give birth to Maya!'

She looks scared. She looks worried. She looks terribly, terribly sorry as she catches my eye. But she doesn't look like she's lying.

'I found her,' she says. 'In the showers at school. At first I thought she was a dream, my sweet, sweet dream.'

I can't move as the words sink in.

'I told everyone I hid the pregnancy, but really I was never pregnant.'

My mum is not my mum. She wasn't pregnant when she was thirteen. She wasn't pregnant at all.

The doctor looks at me. Dave looks at me. I think I might collapse.

But instead I turn and run.

Chapter 36

I'm running through the long white corridors with tears streaming down my face. Everyone's looking at me but no one stops me. In hospital, I guess people cry all the time. But they don't know what's just happened – no one could ever guess. My mum is not my real mum. She found me and passed me off as her own. She lied to everyone and she lied to me.

I've always wondered about my real dad because I've never met him. It turns out I've never met my real mum either.

I turn corners as I run. My heart is beating so fast that I have to speed up to keep up with its rhythm.

Finally I see the big double doors of the exit and I head for them. I have no idea where I'm going and I don't really care.

I am not Maya Andrews. So who am I?

'No running in the hospital!' yells a woman at reception.

That doesn't make me stop though. The automatic doors open for me as I sprint out into the car park. But my vision's blurry – partly from the tears and partly from the shock.

'Maya!' Someone calls my name as I race past the parked ambulances.

But I don't want to speak to anyone. I hear footsteps running up behind me.

'Maya,' the voice says again. This time he grabs my shoulders. I try to shake him off but he's too strong for me. I'm hit by the smell of washing powder.

'Let me go!' I shout.

But he doesn't. I stop. I'm panting so hard that it's difficult to breathe.

'Maya, what's the matter?' Luke asks. 'Are you OK? Why are you at the hospital?'

My mouth flaps but nothing comes out. 'I . . . I . . . I . . .'

He wraps his arms round me and holds me tight.

'You're shaking,' he says, and he sounds worried. 'Do you need a doctor?'

'No!' I say. 'I can't go back in there. My mum's

in there.' There's a huge pull on my heart when I say the word *mum*, because she's not my mum at all.

He hugs me again.

'Luke,' says a woman's gentle voice, 'is everything OK?'

I look up from Luke's chest and see a woman that I sort of recognize. She looks really tired, deep circles under her eyes. But she looks sweet and kind too. Now I remember; she's Luke's mum.

'Are you OK, love?' she asks me.

I have no words to describe what I am, so we're left in silence for a second. Luke's mum is holding Raphael's hand. Raphael smiles at me, and weirdly I find myself smiling back.

'Mum,' says Luke, 'can you tell them I'll be in in a minute?'

Luke's mum considers this and obviously decides that I need Luke more than she does right now.

'OK,' she says. 'But we can't keep Dr Hayward waiting.'

She leads Raphael into the hospital.

Luke takes me by the arm and we walk over to a patch of grass and a few trees across from the car park. He sits me down on a bench and puts his arm round me.

'Do you want to talk about it?' he asks.

'I don't know.'

I say nothing for a moment.

'I just found out that my mum isn't who she said she is,' I say slowly. 'She's been lying to me my whole life.'

Luke looks thoughtful. He sighs before he says, 'Thing is, with adults, they're just like us: they don't know what they're doing most of the time either.'

I play with my hands as I try to understand his words.

'Is your mum a good mum?' he asks.

'Yes.'

'Has she always loved you?'

I nod, and well up with tears again.

'Well, then. I guess what I'm saying is that whatever she did, she did it for a reason. She might not be right, but you know that she'd never hurt you on purpose.'

I do know my mum loves me. And with all the awful stuff I've done over the last month I can understand people doing bad things for their own warped reasons. 'Don't take her side,' I say. But I'm only joking, and he knows it. 'Do you have to go now?' I ask.

He winces and nods. 'We have an appointment,' he says.

'For Raphael?'

'No, actually,' he says. 'For me.'

'Oh,' I say. I'm not brave enough to ask more. I know so much about Luke, about Raphael, and about the pills he takes. I don't want to lie and pretend I don't.

'Sorry I've been such a freak,' he says. 'The thing is, I didn't want anyone to find out the truth.'

'The truth?' I say, in a way that means he only has to tell me if he wants to.

'You know the rumour about me?' he asks.

'Which one? I've heard loads.'

This makes him laugh. 'You must have heard about how I bullied some kid at my old school. Beat him up so badly that I put him in hospital for six months. That I was kicked out and sent to Mount Selwyn.'

'Errr . . .' I'm not sure whether I should admit it or not.

'I know you know that rumour, because I spread it myself,' he says. 'But it's not true.'

'It's not?'

I didn't do what they think I did . . .

'*I* was the boy that was in hospital for six months.'

'Oh.'

'There were these kids a few years above teasing Raphael and pushing him around. They thought they were cool – people like Karmella and Rochelle and Ben Sands and Gary Cohen – but they were the most uncool freaks.'

Starting with the freaks who are completely uncool.

'I tried to step in and protect him, but I wasn't as strong as I am now.' He's clearly reliving the moment in his head. 'Raphael got away with a black eye, but they pushed me to the floor and started kicking me. I ended up with five broken bones, one of them my femur – my thigh bone. I was in hospital for six months and I still have to take painkillers.'

'Oh.' His pills are for his leg, not to stop him from going insane. But one thing doesn't make sense. 'So why do you want people to think you're like them?'

'If everyone thinks I'm hard and mean they won't start on my brother,' he says. 'It's a bit rubbish to have everyone think I'm a bully –' he throws a glance back in the direction his mum and brother went – 'but Raphael deserves it.'

277

Luke's secret is falling into place and I realize that I was right not to be afraid of him.

'Maya, are you OK?' he asks, looking at his watch. 'Only my mum will kill me if I'm late.'

'You go,' I say.

'Not until we've called someone,' he says. 'Where's your phone? Let's call your best friend and see if she can come and get you.'

My phone has seven missed calls from Dave but I ignore that, think about it for a second, and start writing a text:

> I know I have been horrible and I'm so sorry, Frankie.
> But I'm having such a terrible time. You are my best
> friend and I really, really need you right now.

I press send and sigh, knowing I've lost her and it's useless.

But two seconds later my phone rings.

'Hiya, Maya,' says Frankie, sounding so sweet and worried about me. 'Are you OK?'

'No,' I howl.

'Where are you?' she says. 'I'm coming to get you.'

I feel so relieved. I breathe out one long, big breath. 'Frankie, thank you.'

Frankie sighs. 'What do you think *forever* means?' she says. 'I am your best friend forever.

278

We might fall out from time to time, but nothing's going to change that.'

And I'm so glad it's true.

I tell her I'm at the hospital and she manages to restrain herself and not ask what's going on.

'I'll call Zeba too,' she says. 'It sounds like you need your two best friends.'

I am so lucky to have two best friends.

Luke gets up. 'I really have to go now, Maya,' he says. 'Call me later and let me know that you're OK, yeah?'

Maybe, after this is all done, I might even end up with three best friends.

Chapter 37

I have never eaten Persian food before, but it's really good. Partly because I haven't eaten in over twenty-four hours. We're all sat round Zeba's kitchen table – Zeba, Frankie, me, and Zeba's mum, dad, older brother and his wife – eating a banquet. This is the first time I have been round to Zeba's house and it's really nice; we're at a long dining table in a conservatory, where the hot food has made condensation on the cold glass.

'Thanks for having me, Mrs Khan,' I say.

'You're welcome, Maya,' she says. She smiles at me, but there is pity in her eyes.

'Congratulations,' says Mr Khan, coming in from the hallway where he just answered the phone. 'Your mother's had a healthy baby boy.' He says it in a way that no one has ever said *congratulations* before. Like he's not sure. 'Mother and baby are both doing well.'

I raise my water glass and everyone raises theirs too.

'Cheers,' I say.

'Cheers!' says Zeba, and the rest of her family join in.

I've asked if I can stay with Zeba. Mr and Mrs Khan have spoken to Gran, and everyone's agreed it's a good idea, until the dust settles and we're ready to talk about everything.

It's a bit awkward round the table because such a massive thing has happened. And not just for me, but for Zeba too. Zeba's wearing goth make-up and clothes in front of her parents for the first time. She's decided not to lie any more.

'Maya,' says Mr Khan, trying to get back to safer ground, 'it was very good of you to arrange that poetry competition.'

'Zeba and Frankie did it with me,' I say.

'It was my pleasure,' says Frankie.

'Sorry that you were misled in thinking that Zeba was going to win,' I say.

'We're glad we came,' says Mrs Kahn. 'At least now we know why Zeba takes such a big bag to school every day.'

Zeba cringes. 'You don't mind, do you, Mum?'

'No,' she says. 'It's natural for a girl your age to like clothes . . .'

Mr Kahn nods along. 'I will have to make one rule though.'

'What?' asks Zeba, preparing herself for the worst.

'You can only listen to that awful music with your headphones!' he says, and laughs.

We all laugh too, but Zeba looks insulted. 'You lot have no taste. We are starting regular VDP appreciation lessons, every evening at eight!' she says, and I wonder if she actually means it.

'Mr Swift, the poet, read your poem, Zeba, and he thought it was really good,' I tell her.

Zeba beams. 'Really?'

'Yes,' I say. 'He said it was excellent and it showed lots of potential.'

'*Potential?!* Ha!' Zeba scoffs. 'My poem is absolutely brilliant already!'

We all smile at her hissy fit.

'Oh dear,' Frankie says. 'Looks like we have a poetry diva on our hands!'

'I'd love to hear it, darling,' says Zeba's mum. 'Will you read it out for us now?'

'Do you have a spare copy?' I ask her.

'Are you crazy?' she says. 'I know it off by heart!'

She stands and clears her throat. '"All Made Up",' she says, 'by Manar Sakina Adiba Khan.'

Frankie and I share a secret giggle at Zeba's expense, but then Zeba takes a deep breath, we all fall silent and she starts:

> Sitting at my mirror,
> staring at my face,
> plaster on the warpaint,
> so nothing's out of place.
>
> First I start with cover-up,
> cover up my lies.
> Then apply the colour
> to the shadows on my eyes.
>
> Outline the lips with liner
> so no one hears their words,
> gloss over them with sparkle
> and their meaning starts to blur.
>
> I must have concealer,
> the foundation of the truth,
> they might guess, but I'll not confess
> and they'll never have the proof.

While I perfect the visage
just after I wake up
no one sees the girl who's me
just the person I make up.

When she's finished we let the words sink in for a second, then clap like mad.

Mrs Khan gets up from the table. 'That was lovely, darling,' she says. 'Why don't I clear these plates?' Then she sniffs and runs from the room.

Zeba looks at her dad, who says, 'You are a very talented poet, *azizam*.'

'Thanks, Dad,' she says. 'I was thinking of sending it to VDP, to see if they want to use it as lyrics.'

'Go on, you girls,' her dad says. 'Get upstairs. Leave us in peace before she starts singing one of their songs!'

We all push our chairs back and run upstairs.

Frankie goes first, then Zeba and then me. But I'm walking slower than the other two, looking at the pictures on the walls. So many show family gatherings that it makes me think.

We pile into Zeba's room, where a bed and two mattresses are laid out side by side. The other two jump on to Zeba's bed while I stand there. They're ready to do normal things, like try on clothes and make-up and talk about boys. No more of this secrets stuff – it's too intense.

'Did I tell you?' Zeba asks. 'After you left the poetry competition Mark Nowicki stood up and publicly called Karmella a liar. He says he never kissed Rochelle. Him and Amanda are back on!'

'That's great,' I say.

'And,' Zeba continues, 'Rochelle has changed her relationship status on Facebook!'

'Really?' asks Frankie. 'To what?'

'In a relationship . . . with Billy Beckworth!'

Frankie gets up and whoops with joy. 'That's great news!' She high-fives Zeba. 'She obviously doesn't care what evil Karmella thinks any more!' Then they both turn to high-five me but they are stopped by the expression on my face.

'You know what?' I say. 'I don't think Karmella is evil.'

Frankie guffaws.

'She *is* evil,' I correct myself. 'But she's also sad and lonely like everyone else. She just deals with it in the wrong way. And she's so cool that everyone likes her and lets her get away with it.'

Frankie frowns and looks thoughtful. 'Maybe you're right, but I'm not sure.'

'What do you mean?'

'I think there are people who are cool and there are people who are nice. Both are popular, but not everyone *likes* the cool people.'

Frankie might be on to something there.

'I know which I would rather be,' she says.

Finally I know that too.

'Well, I have a surprise for you both,' says Zeba.

'What?' asks Frankie.

'It's something that I've been working on on my own, but I think you'll be impressed.'

'Tell us,' I say.

'I've found Hillary Randle,' she says.

'What?' I feel as if all the air has been squeezed from my lungs.

'WHAT!?' shouts Frankie. 'When? How? Are you sure? I thought we said no more secrets!'

'This isn't a secret, it's a *surprise*! Totally different.'

I sit down on the bed and fight back my tears. 'We have to talk to her,' I say.

Both of them look at me, clearly wondering why we have to speak to this old woman from ages ago, and clearly wondering why I'm doubled over at the end of Zeba's bed.

There is still one secret left to solve.

'I'm the same age as Mum when she found me and she chose to keep me. It must have been so hard for her.' I gulp.

'She must love you very much,' Frankie says.

I hadn't thought about it like that. I'm looking at Frankie in her My Little Pony tracksuit top, and I'm amazed that they even make My Little Pony clothes for people over five years old. I'm glad she hasn't changed. Frankie can be very wise sometimes.

'But why do we have to talk to Hillary Randle?' Zeba asks.

I look up at them with tears in my eyes. 'Because I've been thinking about it.' I take a deep breath. 'And I'm pretty sure she's my mother.'

Epilogue

Two months later . . .

I get out of the car first and Mum follows. Neither of us says anything as she hands baby Patrick to Dave, her new diamond engagement ring sparkling on her hand. The baby squirms a little and then goes straight back to sleep. He's such a good baby and I love him so much, probably because I'm his favourite thing in the world. He gave his first ever smile when he was looking at me.

'Are you sure you don't want me to come with you?' asks Dave.

I'm terrified, and part of me would like Dave to be there to make sure everything's OK. But this feels like something that me and Mum should do on our own. The social worker who's handling our case – Miss Carmichael – said that would be for the best.

'We'll be here if you need us,' Dave says to me, but I know that he's talking to Mum too.

Mum looks awful. This is almost as big a day for her as it is for me.

'Good luck,' says Dave.

'Good luck!' screams the mob from the back. Dave had to hire a people carrier to take us from our new house in Greenford up to Manchester, because as soon as Frankie insisted on coming for moral support, Zeba did too, and Luke wanted to come as well.

I shoot them a weak smile.

Mum and I turn towards the small terraced house. I take Mum's hand and we start up the path. 'Are you OK, Mum?'

'I should be asking you that,' she says. 'I know you've had to look after me a lot, Maya. Well, not any more. I'm your . . .' She stops herself from saying *mum*. 'I mean, I'm the adult.'

'You're my mum, Mum,' I say. She's loved me and looked after me from almost the moment I was born. Yes, she's made mistakes, but she was young and she's only human. 'You've always been here,' I say.

'How are you feeling?' she says.

'I feel sick.'

I know she knows that we're coming, but what if she's changed her mind and she doesn't want to meet me after all? What if she left me in the girls' showers because she didn't want to know me? And what if she still doesn't?

Mum bends down and gives me a big hug.

'What if, when she meets me, she thinks I'm a disappointment?' I say.

Mum pushes me gently back by my shoulders and looks me in the eye. 'Anyone who knows you feels lucky to know you. You are marvellous.'

But she has to say that because she's my mum.

'Are you ready?' she asks.

I nod.

Mum knocks on the door. The inside of my mouth feels dry like concrete. My legs are wobbly and I don't know if I'm going to be able to stand here for long.

I hear movement inside – footsteps – and through the mottled glass in the front door I see a shadow coming towards us.

I swallow, trying to work out what to say.

The door opens a crack, and I see a woman, a bit older than Mum, with blue eyes like mine and blonde hair like mine and a definite bump in her nose.

Hillary Randle, my mother, stands in front of me. She looks at me and her face crumples.

'Hi,' I say. A bit lame, but it's the best I can do.

Her eyes are full of tears and her lips tremble as she speaks.

'Baby?'

THE END

Interview with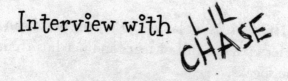

Hi Lil! So, are you any good at keeping secrets?

Yes! That's what good friends do.

But if it's a *really* juicy secret I'm bursting to tell . . . well, that's what my dog is for. If Stella (my Staffy cross) could talk, she'd be a canine Locker 62.

What would you have done if you had been assigned Locker 62?

Definitely try to find out who wrote what, and if someone was in love with someone else I would matchmake. But knowing everyone's deepest darkest secrets is quite a lot of responsibility. Eventually I think I'd tell a teacher.

Lots of people in your book feel different, or like 'freaks' compared to other people. Did you ever feel like that? Or were you the super-cool popular girl?

'*Super-cool girl*'? Ha! Good one!

I was in a popular group when I was at school, but I was the least cool girl in it . . . which made me feel even more of a freak.

Recently I went through all the old letters that friends had sent when I was a teenager. Almost every one said how weird/stupid/crazy/ugly/out of place we felt. It's sad because we were all feeling the same way, which meant we weren't out of place at all.

Did you always want to write books, or was it something you became interested in as an adult?

I wanted to be a million things when I was young – an actress, a forensic pathologist, an opera singer – but one thing that never went away was writing. My first book – *Boys for Beginners* – was actually based on a story I wrote when I was ten, called 'Gwynnie Goes Girlie'. When I say 'based on', I really mean 'stolen from': it was exactly the same story. I just polished it up and got rid of the terrible drawings.

Where do you get the ideas for your books?

Boys for Beginners I found in my parents' attic. *Secrets, Lies & Locker 62* was harder to come up with.

It came from two pretty bad ideas: one about best friends who put their secrets in a piggy bank, and the other about a girl at military school who had her girlie things hidden in a pink locker. I combined the ideas, changed the piggy bank of secrets to a locker full of secrets, and *Locker 62* was born!

And finally ... tell us a secret!

I have a not-so-secret crush on all the boys I write about in my books, and the biggest crush on Luke Marshall. The secret is that Luke is based on a boy I know.

That boy's name? There's no way I'm telling you!

For more about Lil and her books visit
www.lilchase.co.uk

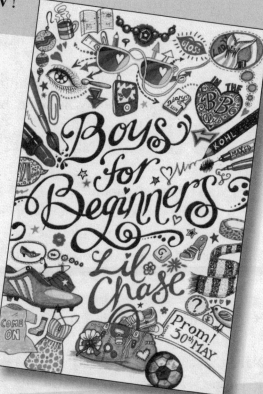

Gwynnie is a real tomboy, but when she turns fourteen she realizes she might want to be more than just friends with a certain Charlie Notts . . .

Charlie says, 'Hey, Gwynnie, I don't have your number.'

OK, it's not the completely romantic way that I'd hoped he'd ask for my number, but he's still asked for my number.

He gets out his phone. 'Call me and I'll save it.'

'Er, I don't have a mobile yet.' This is why I need a mobile phone. Mobile phones were invented exactly for moments like these.

'Oh.' Charlie, like everyone, is shocked by this fact.

Jenny cuts in as if she's trying to be helpful. 'It's OK, Charlie, Gwynnie can always get you on my phone.'

'Nah, that's cool,' says Charlie. 'I'll take your home phone.' He starts tapping at his keypad. 'Hang on a sec, I'll add you to my "Mates" group.'

Charlie Notts has just said that I'm his mate! This is fantastic. I wonder if he means *mates* like friends, or *mates* like mates on nature shows.

He gives me his phone to type in my number. There don't seem to be any girls' names in his phone. This is great! I am the only girl who Charlie wants in his phone.

Hang on a minute. Doesn't he have Jenny's number?

'Do you want to enter Jenny's number after I put in mine?' I ask.

'I already have it,' he says.

'But it's not here,' I say.

Something about the way Charlie sort of blushes and looks at the floor tells me that I'm not going to like what I am about to hear. 'No, er . . . this is my "Mates" group. I put Jenny into my "Girls" group.' Jenny beams, but when Charlie turns to look at her she drops the smile. 'Sorry, Jenny, I hope you don't mind.'

Jenny nods in a kind of forgiving *that's OK* kind of way.

I am destroyed. Charlie doesn't think of me as a girl. He thinks of me as a mate! And obviously not a nature-show-type mate.

'I can put you in under "Girls" instead, Gwynnie. If you like.' He grabs the phone off me and gets to the Girls group, then hands the phone back to me.

I am astonished at how many girls he has in his phone. It just makes it all the worse that he doesn't think of me as one of them.

'Whatever,' I say, and type in my number. 'Anyway, see you at school tomorrow.' I give him back his phone and run away from them, not able to even say goodbye.

Maybe if I was more ladylike then he wouldn't just think of me as a mate. Maybe Kevin's right: I have to act more like a girl if I want guys to notice me.

Will it work? Maybe it won't. I'll have to give up football and Xbox and start hanging around with all those stupid BB girls. But then again, it would be so amazing to be Charlie's girlfriend, to kiss him, to go out on dates and stuff.

OK . . . That's it . . . I am going to do it.

Gwynnie Lewis is going girlie!